NIGHTS IN BERLIN

NIGHTS IN BERLIN

A Francis Bacon Mystery

JANICE LAW

MYSTERIOUSPRESS.COM

INTEGRATED MEDIA

NEW YORK

Cover design by Mauricio Díaz

978-1-5040-2616-1

Published in 2016 by MysteriousPress.com/Open Road Integrated Media, Inc.
180 Maiden Lane
New York, NY 10038
www.mysteriouspress.com
www.openroadmedia.com

To my friends at Fletcher Memorial Library

As a teenager, the Anglo-Irish painter Francis Bacon was sent to Weimar Berlin with an uncle, but that fact has been surrounded by pure fiction. The characters and events are wholly imaginary and any resemblance to persons living or dead is truly coincidental.

NIGHTS IN BERLIN

CHAPTER ONE

Dear Francis,

So they are sending you among the godless Huns. You will need to look sharp, dear boy, and mind yourself. They say a lot about Berlin, and I don't doubt for a moment that most of it is true, as the city is full of heathens.

Still, a trip to the continent is an education in itself. Remember that a young gentleman must be educated, and travel is undoubtedly the least painful means. Since you have not shown much taste for school, this may prove to be just the ticket. I do hope so, dear boy, for you have great capabilities.

Now, as for getting home, I wish to see you beyond all things, but even if you were allowed back before your trip, I would not be in residence. Young Eddie is ready for school, the girls are away, and a nanny is, in your father's opinion, superfluous. I have received my two weeks' notice and must look for another position.

As soon as you are settled in Berlin, send me a note in care of my sister in Brighton. She will forward mail to me.

Keep a stout heart and a bright face, and never doubt your nan loves you.

XXXX

I folded up the letter, already well creased from reading, and put it back into my jacket pocket. Nan was leaving, and with her went the last possible reason for me to return to Ireland. As far as I can determine after nearly seventeen years of observation, my dear Nan is the one and only person who is always glad to see me. For the rest of the family, I have been the cuckoo in the nest. My main thought has been to take flight, and theirs, to see the back of me.

Sitting on my trunk waiting for Uncle Lastings and anticipating the unknown delights of Berlin, I was feeling sorry for myself. This is something Nan always discouraged, self-pity being, in her mind, the eighth deadly sin. Hence my rereading of a letter that I already knew by heart. *Count your blessings, Francis*, she used to say, and yes, the last few months had brought some definite advantages: I was in London. Therefore, I was not in Ireland, which means I was not surrounded by the horses and dogs that cause my eyes to swell up and my lungs to close. I was also out of reach of my father, who dislikes me.

My mother was mildly concerned about my conduct; my brothers and sisters, indifferent. But Father outright disapproved, and having dispatched me from home several months ago, he had now taken it into his head to reform me. From what?

you may ask. Trifles, really. I was too fond of certain boys at school, hence my return to the family home, and then too partial to trying out Mother's underwear and rouge, hence my exile to London.

As Nan used to say, neither was *a hanging offense by a long chalk*, but I had been living by my wits in Soho ever since. Happily, liking boys there was no crime, makeup was all the rage, and my face, considered homely back at the manse, passed muster quite nicely. A good thing, too, as my allowance of three pounds a month did not stretch very far. Certainly not to decent dinners and glasses of wine and nice clothes.

I had learned to make use of my assets, and I'd landed on my feet. Or to take Father's point of view, I'd *set out on the road to ruin*. Now I was to be rescued by Uncle Lastings, who would return me to home and family as a model boy in the soldierly mode—my uncle, late of the royal Berkshires, being in Father's words *the right sort to make a man of you.*

That's the way Father talked, and tedious it was, too, what with alternate references to the turf—he ran an unsuccessful race-training stable—and the military. You'd think he spent the Great War on the western front instead of in an office in London, for he was always going on about the *need for guts* and a *willingness to go over the top*, all delivered with a good deal of shouting and stamping and blows left and right.

I was afraid his notion was to turn me into a similarly roaring bully. Good luck with that. Men like my father caught my eye, but I certainly didn't want to be one of them. No siree, Bob. So I was determined that Uncle Lastings would have his work cut out for him. He could start by paying my landlady, although I had five pounds in my inner jacket pocket, thanks to a gentleman from Cyprus who took me to the Savoy and was generous afterward. But that was for me to know.

The bell rang downstairs. I straightened my shoulders—how many times had Father screamed "Shoulders back!" at me?—and got ready for my uncle. If he was going to reform me, he was going to pay for the pleasure.

·   ·   ·

Dear Nan,

I am settled in Berlin in the Adlon Hotel, the best in the city. The bed curtains are silk and room service comes on silver trays. It's beyond comfy and quite a change from my last digs at school! I am going about and seeing everything—believe me, there is plenty to see—and visiting all the galleries and museums, full of wild, wild stuff: green faces and purple horses and amazing etchings and drawings of grotesque heads and bodies—such as one sees on every sidewalk, because even on Unter der Linden, there are beggars and war wounded. Nonetheless, I feel quite at home, and Uncle Lastings is seeing that I learn a bit of German.

I stopped right there. Every word was true, especially that I did feel at home. I did, I did! In Ireland I was a sinful freak, if not an outright criminal, and even in London, I was on thin ice most nights. *Au contraire*, in Berlin, my little indulgences passed without notice in what Uncle Lastings terms "the welcome circus of depravity." My uncle had a way with words.

The difficulty was that mine didn't go far enough. I would have liked to tell Nan a bit more about my uncle and nighttime Berlin, which, believe me, presented some sights. I chewed the end of my pen and thought things over, because I had the feeling that Uncle Lastings, who always volunteered to mail my letters—*I can save you the postage, Francis*—read them. Too bad, as Uncle was a big part of what made Berlin so fascinating. Appearance, first: He was bigger than my father, probably six feet and a couple inches; he had a square red face and a lumpy nose above a mustache like General Kitchener's; and he walked with a military strut, which helped conceal that he had put on some unmilitary pounds since he last went *over the top*, which I gathered he did.

Unlike Father, my uncle didn't have much to say about the war, having seen and heard enough of it. As he said to me the very first day we met, *I'll be damned if I'll do anything from here on out but fuck around and enjoy myself.* His motto, exactly, and one he lived up to daily, if not hourly. I was lucky, I realized, to get him to pay off my landlady!

But Uncle Lastings always played a long game, as I learned almost as soon as we were on the boat train headed for the coast and our continental sleeper to Berlin. *So, Francis,* he had said and dropped his hand on my knee, *the grand tour commences, eh?*

I took a better look at him then. There he sat, red-faced and clearly ex-army and just the sort to straighten out what Father has taken to calling his *nancy-boy son.* But what was this? His

hand had migrated upward, and was that a most unmilitary
twinkle in his eye? I believe it was.

"Oh," I said, for I have learned how to make myself agreeable,
"I believe we will get along famously."

And we had. I had no problem with going to bed with
Uncle Lastings, who certainly knew what he was about in that
department. It was rather in other departments that my uncle
gave me pause. I wondered how he afforded the Adlon Hotel
and where he went afternoons when he was off on business and
who the mysterious gents who showed up at odd hours and
phoned him from the fancy bar downstairs were. He couldn't
have been sleeping with all of them—well, he could have been
theoretically, given his appetite and stamina—but I thought he
really was on some sort of mission, and I got bad feelings about
his associates, fit young men with thin, tanned faces and wild
eyes. They were not Berliners; they were there on business.

And not what seemed to be the main business of the moment,
either, which was the incredibly specialized flesh trade, offering something for every imaginable taste. The whores and rent
boys came out at dusk to claim their turf according to their ser-
vices, while lights went on in the upper rooms of even the most
respectable-looking housing blocks. Before you knew it, there
were streams of patrons at the front doors and jazz or tangoes on
the gramophones.

"The sovereign power of money over morals," said Uncle
Lastings, who headed off at night to the various clubs, semire-
spectable and otherwise. He was fond of the Resi, with its table
telephones, all the better to proposition some darling on the other

side of the room. Watching my uncle in the flirtatious mode was almost entertainment enough. Almost, but I didn't need to be the wallflower at the party. While Uncle tried to charm some woman with money, I casted my eye among the younger waiters and the boys lined up outside who fancied their chances. Yes, I'd say evening was fine, if occasionally hard on the wallet.

It was afternoon that was beginning to concern me. We got up late, as you might imagine. Breakfast in bed. Very satisfactory. Then Uncle took what he called his constitutional—a brisk walk in the park—while I took myself off to the galleries, where the paintings were nothing like the tame stuff done at home. Artists in Berlin felt free to express themselves and favored the exaggerated and grotesque; they were trying to catch what was on the streets right then. I didn't know why I was so fascinated when everything they were painting was just outside, but I was. *How does it get done? How to put the world into paint and onto canvas? How to turn emotion into color?* That was what I would have liked to know, although I was not sure why just yet.

I only returned to the hotel after the galleries closed. Sometimes Uncle Lastings was down in the bar, deep in conversation with one of his associates. Occasionally, two or three of them would be up in our room, the air brown with the smoke of their pipes and cigars, forcing me to take my dodgy lungs and retreat to the winter garden or the ornate lobby. After these meetings, my uncle was in one of two moods: expansive and cheerful, and we would head out for a fancy dinner and champagne, or surly, and he would go off alone and I would eat on the cheap.

Sometimes he disappeared for a night or two, and when he

did, he took his Webley revolver with him. Otherwise, it lay in the bottom of his case. He made frequent trips to one of the banks, and he carried very few marks—*rely on the pound sterling, my boy*—so whatever business he was doing must've been in hard currency. And quite profitable, too, because even with the power of the pound, the Adlon was expensive, not to mention Uncle Lastings's other diversions.

Though jovial and talkative about most things, my uncle was silent on his purpose for being in Berlin until early one afternoon when we were walking near the Alexanderplatz. The bustle of the city and the noise of the trolley and cabs were suddenly interrupted by a sound like a rising wind that soon became singing voices, accompanied by the rhythmic thump of marching boots on cobblestones.

"Here they come," said Uncle Lastings with a kind of relish.

"Who?"

"The Bolshies, of course. Damn Reds. Reason we're here, boy! To fight the advance guard of the godless." He pulled me back from the street as a mob of men and boys, eight abreast, marched by, shouting for jobs and food and death to speculators, all beneath a small forest of red flags and banners painted with slogans. There were songs, too, bellowed out in unison, and the marchers' feet rang out so clearly that people threw their windows open and leaned out and cheered.

Uncle Lastings, however, seemed to be waiting for something else. He kept scanning the spectators and looking down the side streets. The main marchers had just passed us when we heard the sound of breaking glass ahead. Uncle Lastings craned his neck as rocks started bouncing into the street, thrown by men who were coming out of the neighboring beer halls.

"The Vikings," Uncle Lastings said with satisfaction. "Or maybe the Brownshirts." He grabbed my arm and pulled me into an alleyway. "Head down."

Within minutes, the orderly, seemingly irresistible march began to fragment. The songs broke off and the marching cadence dissolved as shouting men ran first one way and then another, advancing, retreating, swirling into fights and throwing whatever came to hand. Anyone who fell or was isolated was instantly set upon by men with clubs, or the splintered poles of the flags, or trampled beneath heavy boots. Several bleeding combatants took refuge behind the metal bins in our alley before we heard a bugle and the clatter, clink, and rattle of cavalry, familiar to me from my childhood near the Curragh. The mob flowed away in thunderous waves of running feet, pursued by saber-wielding horsemen.

I found the march and its aftermath scary but curiously exciting, as if the prints and paintings I'd been admiring had come to life, their truth revealed. I was eager to get back out onto the street, but Uncle Lastings shook his head.

"Stragglers are in danger in no-man's-land," he said with a chilly and distant look in his eyes. So we waited.

After a while, he lit his pipe, and once he had communed with the tobacco, we stepped out of our hiding place. The street was strewn with glass and torn flags and slick in places with blood and manure. Some of the injured were still lying dazed in the gutter; others were being helped to safety by young women

who came out of the apartments and tenements, some with bandages, as if this was no more than they'd been expecting.

Reason we're here, my uncle had said, and this seemed like a
good chance to ask him just what he meant.

"The men you meet—are they involved?" I asked.

"Of course," said Uncle Lastings. "A new force in Europe is
very much needed." He spat on the sidewalk. "Berlin's a Red city.
It pulls Prussia with it, next thing you know you've got a Bolshie
state on the French border. And the Frogs are half-Red already,
so time to make a stand."

I couldn't see much difference between the groups of street
fighters, or between the marchers and the rough and seedy-
looking gents who met with my uncle. "They were throwing
rocks," I said.

"The reason I'm at work, my boy. Rocks aren't going to do it,
not when the Reds have the numbers. Firepower and organization—those are the keys, and the Society for a Christian Europe
is the means for both."

"The Society for a Christian Europe?" It sounded like a tract
society, one of those outfits with religious leaflets that occasionally descended into Soho to warn that sex leads to damnation. I
was already pretty well immune to that notion. "Does the society
really exist?"

He gave me a look, and, at first, I thought he was going to be
angry, that I had overstepped and now would learn nothing. But
he gave a little cynical smirk. "Such a skeptical boy! No wonder
Eddy sent you off with me. Of course it exists; and I am its Berlin
agent." He pulled out an official-looking metal badge.

"What do you do as the Berlin agent?"

"Well, now, that is another matter. I assist the society by funneling money to the worthy, for a commission, of course."

Of course, along with rooms at the Adlon and nightly visits to the sex clubs and cafés and fancy restaurants. "And the men you meet?"

"Gentlemen on the right, interested in arms. Which I can also arrange."

"For a commission?"

"Naturally. It's a delicate business, which, Francis, is why I have been pleased to have you along. Chaperoning a young nephew around Berlin lends credibility in certain quarters."

Although I thoroughly enjoyed nightspots like the Resi and the transvestite employees of the Eldorado, I was not sure they could be considered innocent amusements. Not by a society aimed at Christian Europe.

He must have read that on my face because he nodded after a moment and said, "Certainly the society *could* exist. Remember, Francis, whatever man can imagine, can exist. "

That seemed to be good advice in Berlin. And a bit of a warning.

CHAPTER TWO

Dear Nan,

Uncle Lastings is off on business, so I have the run of the Hotel Adlon, including all the behind-the-scenes areas, thanks to a hall boy I've befriended. Fritz wants to become a waiter and is keen to learn English. I can oblige, so I'm getting to know the hotel inside and out. Good thing, too, as my uncle has been very busy lately, writing up reports for the society and taking trips to other German cities. I have not been invited, but that doesn't bother me because Berlin has enough interest for a dozen towns.

Just between us, I think Uncle Lastings is in some difficulties. He's been talking lately of being "down the rabbit hole," which doesn't sound good at all. At the moment, he has hopes of some National Socialist fellow who is due in town from Munich. Uncle thinks they might be the sort for the society to support in their fight against the Bolsheviks.

More to the point was that Uncle Lastings thought *this Goebbels Johnny* would be a sure pigeon. *Fresh out of the beer halls, my boy! They've named him Gauleiter of Berlin, and he's going to need money to go with the title.*

True enough, but when I mentioned that was a mighty big Red march we'd seen the other day, Uncle Lastings just rubbed his hands. "Wouldn't be worth our while otherwise," he said. "Ever since the Republic scuttled the Freikorps, the right-wing outfits have been looking for funds and supplies. They've got to have newspapers and magazines and cash for their fighters. With a little luck and my commission, I avoid the rabbit hole, Francis, and get the old exchequer into the black."

Which would have made sense, if there really had been a Society for Christian Europe instead of some gullible types back home who were trusting Uncle Lastings with contributions to fight the Reds. Another nice question was how he was going to profit from a bunch of street fighters who didn't look like they had more than the clothes they stood up in.

But if nothing else, Uncle Lastings kept, as he put it, *a lot of irons in the fire.* Besides his political thugs, he was always on the lookout for the wealthy and philanthropic, who were usually women of a certain age, girth, and income. As he told me more than once, *Options are vital to strategy, and the nemesis of action is rigidity.* Useful ideas, and he certainly lived by them. His plans were all improvised, and although we were still staying at the Adlon and hitting the best clubs, his strategy appeared more and more uncertain. At least to me.

My uncle, however, returned from his trip to Bavaria in a

buoyant mood. "It's like a comic opera down there, my boy—matching shirts and military drills and slogans. The order for the flags alone would have made my fortune. Although a *viable* alternative to the Bolsheviks is what we need," he said, pulling a long face and quoting one of the society's pamphlets. "In the meantime, a chap has to make a living." He threw back his head and laughed and treated me to a bottle of good champagne. I was developing a taste for that.

So, as Nan would say, everything was lovely in the garden—until a week later when the gauleiter arrived. After considerable difficulties and a long wait, Uncle Lastings met with him and found him lacking. *A miserable little cripple* was his private judgment, an opinion that he soon had to revise, because within days, the city saw numerous brawls and street demonstrations, all provoked by fighters under the red-and-black National Socialist banners.

Uncle Lastings began to look rather serious, even if he stayed out even later at the clubs, refusing, as he put it, to *let private troubles interfere with pleasure*. But one night he was clearly feeling uneasy about an appointment that I assumed must be with some of the new gauleiter's men. My uncle told me to eat at the hotel and not to leave until he called me. This was unprecedented. Then he opened his case and took out the Webley.

"Know anything about these?" he asked me. This was also unprecedented.

I shook my head. Fortunately, Father was not particularly keen on shooting, so marching around the fields with guns has never been part of the program.

"The safety," Uncle Lastings said, pointing. "The trigger."

The weapon was heavy in my hand.

"Put it here." He opened the flat leather case that he used for carrying society documents. "If I call you, bring this. Get a cab no matter what the time. Understand?"

I understood that my uncle was in deep water, but I nodded, and he proceeded to give me the most explicit directions imaginable. He'd be in a right-wing *Lokal*, a bar called the White Cat, and I was to tip the cabbie well to ensure that he would wait.

"But only if I call you, which I'm sure I won't. Excess of caution, my boy, that's all." He put his hat on his head and went to the door, where he said, "You'll be tickety-boo, Francis, see if you're not," before he was off down the corridor.

For some reason, that made me feel more unsettled than even the sight of the Webley, but I decided to follow Uncle Lastings's line and put pleasure, in the form of a fine Adlon dinner, ahead of anxiety. I put on my evening jacket—Uncle Lastings was generous when it came to my appearance—and went downstairs. In the bar off the lobby, I had a glass of wine and chatted with Fritz and Una, he in soup and fish, she in mauve satin, and both looking respectable enough to stay at the hotel. In fact they were employees of a special nature, the Adlon paying them to offer private amusements of one sort or another for guests.

In between times, they and their similarly handsome, similarly elegant colleagues lounged about the lobby or escorted clients to the dining salon. I was tempted to invite Fritz to dinner, but I was afraid Uncle's call might deprive him of his fee.

Too bad. I disliked eating alone, especially since I wasn't as shy as I used to be, especially after a few glasses of wine. Still, I liked the hotel restaurant with its dark wood paneling and the heavy white damask on the round tables, the fine china and silver and the lavish menu. Because I was early and only a few of the older patrons were seated, I got the full treatment from the waiters. I knew most of them well enough to risk my uncertain and slangy German, which amused them a good deal.

After cutlets, roast vegetables, a tart with cream, and several more glasses of Rhine wine, I didn't mind confinement in the hotel, although reading in the lobby proved to be a poor substitute for the films that I love. Just thinking about them made me restless: Garbo and Jannings and costume dramas; the wonders of *Nosferatu* and *Metropolis*; and, best of all, great Russian films like *Battleship Potemkin*. I could watch *Potemkin* once a week indefinitely, no matter what Uncle Lastings said about the Reds.

Sometime after eleven, I returned to our room, convinced that my uncle had finished his meeting and would be rattling his key at any moment. I was taking off my shoes when the phone rang; the deskman told me, in careful English, to meet my uncle promptly. I ordered a cab and said I'd be right down, then caught a glimpse of myself in the large gilt mirror: Dinner attire would never do. I changed my starched shirt and tie for a sweater and my leather jacket. Then I grabbed the envelope heavy with the Webley, and feeling too nervous for the elevator, ran down the stairs and through the lobby to the street.

The White Cat was up north in one of the poor, industrial sectors of the city, a place of smoky works and ancient tenements, a world away from the glittering center. The district was crowded with industries and the workers who ran them, along with the desperate unemployed, the shattered vets, and the war wounded, who emerged daily in the center city with their crutches and canes and ghastly mutilations, some fake but all too many genuine.

The streetlights seemed dimmer once we left the luxury quarters, the streets themselves less crowded with cars and rimmed by gloomy buildings and impenetrable alleys. It seemed a long way before the cab pulled up in front of a low and dimly lit bar with a half-broken neon sign and a badly sketched poster of a naked dancer. I paid the driver, and as Uncle Lastings had instructed, tipped him generously and asked him to wait. He was clearly reluctant. I couldn't blame him. The area felt at once deserted and ominous, with the faint breath of the White Cat's sour music in the air.

"I won't be long," I told him and, tucking the envelope under my arm, I went inside.

Smoke like a London fog. A few lights swimming in the murk. A long bar with a dirty mirror behind, and a few tables to one side. As directed, I ordered a beer, set the envelope on the counter beside me, and scanned the room unobtrusively in the mirror. I did not see Uncle Lastings.

What I saw instead was a room full of the thuggish types we'd seen on both sides of the Reds' march, hungry-looking men, unshaven, half-drunk. If the clubs near the Adlon were all gaiety and excitement, the mood here was sullen. This was the city's underbelly, suffering indigestion. I didn't feel safe, and I wondered how long I was expected to wait. Had something happened to Uncle Lastings? Was my arrival just a feint, a piece of some obscure strategy, or was I waiting for someone else entirely?

I ordered another beer, and I was considering a schnapps to warm me up, when my uncle suddenly sat down on the stool next to mine, met my eye, and gave his head a jerk toward the door. I didn't hesitate. I stood up, and as I did, he slid his hand into the envelope. He had the Webley out and into his jacket in one smooth motion; I hadn't credited him with such finesse.

I went straight outside and signaled my nervous cab driver. The shots came as I was getting into the backseat: one, two, and, a second later, a third and a fourth. The cabbie hit the accelerator before I had the door rightly closed, and it took a good deal of shouting and the waving of a pound note to persuade him to circle the block. I understood him say *Politzei*, and the prospect of police worried me, too, but Uncle Lastings had turned a probable ordeal into valuable experiences. I felt I owed him an exit if he needed one.

At the cost of another pound, the cab driver made a second high-speed circuit down the dodgy little streets, squealing around the corners on two wheels, bouncing over the tram tracks, and squeezing past parked goods trucks. Then I saw a figure running. "Stop! Here! *Halten!*"

A squawk from the brakes. I threw open the door. "Uncle Lastings!"

He waved me away, and I hesitated, the door still open. Then he changed his mind, and with a lunge across the sidewalk, tumbled into the car. A burst of German, and we were away so fast that we were both flung back against the seats.

I expected us to return to the Adlon, but Uncle Lastings had the cab pull up at the *Hauptbahnhof* and signaled for me to get out with him. "I'm sorry, Francis," he said after he had paid the fare and the cabbie roared away, anxious to be rid of us both. "We can't go back." He pulled out a handful of marks and gave them to me. "I'm off. Berlin's impossible for the moment. Do avoid the Adlon, my boy. They've been rather after me for the tab."

With that, he stalked into the station, leaving me on the sidewalk.

I was alone in Berlin with a couple of pounds, a handful of marks, and the clothes I was wearing. I was also, though it didn't register right away, involved in a shooting. With a cabbie who would certainly remember he'd collected me at the Adlon. Whose angry manager would know my name as well as Uncle Lastings's.

I was in what Nan would call a pickle.

CHAPTER THREE

I shivered in the damp breeze, which carried the oily smell of engine smoke. Everything I owned was back at the Adlon, and despite Uncle Lastings's warning, I was tempted to return. On the other hand, those had been real shots, and my uncle's schemes, which had seemed light-hearted if not exactly harmless, now appeared sinister. I kept looking over my shoulder, expecting the police—or, maybe worse, Uncle Lastings's mysterious enemies. Should one or both of them find me, I'd be sunk.

The hotel was another danger, although I wasn't clear what they did to people who couldn't pay for a room. Potato peeling, some other onerous kitchen duty, a quick trip to jail? On the other hand, loitering in the Hauptbahnhof was suspicious, too. I wouldn't care to pick up a soliciting charge on my very first night of independence. No indeed, especially when the clientele at that time of night was dubious. When a large man with a mutilated nose and sores on his face grabbed my arm and started whispering, I hightailed it for the door.

There were cabs at the curb, and telling myself that no one at the hotel could yet know my uncle had vanished, I held up my hand. At the Adlon, I caught my breath and walked in boldly. "*Gute Nacht*, Herr Bacon." That was Albert on the desk, elderly but still stout and handsome in his jacket with the gold braid.

"*Gute Nacht*, Albert," I said and collected my key. All normal. The lobby was as luxurious and smart, the elevators as smooth, the carpeting as rich, the decor as heavy with gilt. With a little effort, I could almost imagine that I'd been asleep in the big four-poster all night and that my rascally uncle was off courting some rich woman or propositioning some pretty boy instead of fleeing a murder charge. Not to mention leaving me penniless and probably implicated. Whoever had shot or been shot, I'd almost certainly delivered the weapon.

Upstairs, the smoke from his cigars lingered along with the fading smell of good breakfasts and furniture polish, but I wasn't feeling sentimental. I immediately turned out his pants and jacket pockets for small change and collected the several pairs of gold cufflinks that were in his case. Other useful advice from Uncle Lastings: *Carry gold. There's always a pawnshop.* He had some silver-mounted brushes, too, and I put them into my own case and threw in my clothes.

What else, what else? Camera. He had a camera, and I found it. A decent Leica. Valuable. I hung its case around my neck. What else? Some documents from the society and a few pamphlets—no profit there. An extra pair of shoes that I was tempted to take for the secondhand market, but no. Safest to leave Uncle Lastings's clothes, suitcase, and shaving stuff. The longer the hotel thought that he was coming back, the safer I'd be. I glanced at the bed, warm and comfortable and full of pleasant memories. *I could sleep til dawn*, I thought, *and no one would be the wiser*. But no. To leave at dawn would be suspicious. To leave now was by no means unprecedented.

The only problem was my case. I could not possibly get it past the eagle-eyed Albert. Could I count on Fritz, my favorite among the hall boys? Fritz, whom I'd given little treats of one sort or another? Maybe, but Fritz was low in the hotel hierarchy. He wouldn't have room keys. Out to the hall. Other valuable advice from Uncle: *Know your terrain and always reconnoiter*. My present terrain was the luxurious hallway of the Adlon. Naturally, the supply closet was locked, to be opened only by the cleaner's big official key. The decorative niche with the oversized vase was not deep enough for a case. That left the hallway windows, flanked on both sides by heavy silk panels. Possible? I thought so.

I fetched my case and, by setting it on end, managed to hide it behind the drapes. Then I put on my jacket and went into the night. It was not too late to find some company, and as luck would have it, I was spotted by a business type, complete with homburg and cane. He had patent leather shoes and wore too much cologne, but his hotel room was comfortable, and by leaving before dawn, I had enough time to catch my friend Fritz.

I stopped at a bakery then waited at the alley beside the hotel until I saw him hurrying in the chilly fog, his hands in the pockets of his thin livery jacket, his face white with cold. I whistled to him, and when he stepped into the alley I, handed him a couple of rolls. "*Frühstück*," I said.

"*Danke*. But what are you doing out here, Francis?"

"A long, sad story." I gave him the short version and explained that my uncle had become a runner. "Left me a note, don't you know," I said before I caught myself. Uncle's turns of phrase were infectious.

"The management will not be happy." Fritz's face was serious, yet I could see that he was not entirely shocked. The workers are Red to a man, Uncle Lastings had said, and I hoped to turn that to account.

"No, so I won't be able to collect my case." I gave him a hopeful look.

Fritz shook his head. "Caught in your room, I lose my job. I am so sorry."

"It's not in the room. I put it behind the drapes at the north window," I said and held out half of one of Uncle's gold cufflink sets.

Fritz closed his hand around it. "I know a place. But case out today. No later."

"As soon as I find a room. I need somewhere cheap out of this district."

Fritz held out his hand for the other cufflink. "Come at six and I take you home with me," he said.

·   ·   ·

Dear Nan,

No more letters to the Adlon. Poste Restante will be the way to go for the near future. Do not worry, I have gotten a room— really much better than the hotel—

That was an exaggeration. Fritz's room was up five flights to the top floor of a once-handsome terraced house. There was a pervasive stink of cabbage soup, fatty sausages, and the over-used and seldom cleaned communal WC. The air was thick with coal smoke from the works. We got the fumes without any compensating heat, and the little warmth the flat's ceramic stove produced was absorbed by Fritz's father, a massive man with a square, scarred face, who sat beside it, wrapped up in an old horse blanket.

Being candid, I added, *except for my friend's father, who occupies the front room. He is a war vet, both eastern and western fronts, and is very lame.*

Also, though I didn't add it yet, very nasty and rather dirty, with perpetual beard stubble, a sullen glance, and a vile temper. A former joiner, he was ruined, Fritz said, in the postwar inflation. Although he still seemed to have some mysterious business going on, poor Fritz, thin and slight, worked day and night to pay the bills while his father drank anything he could get his hands on. In the morning, he was quiet, slyly thinking how he would get alcohol for the day. Once he got it, he was a regular roaring boy, and we'd all be in danger from the bayonet that he kept behind the stove—if he hadn't been hampered by a missing foot and two crutches.

We've had some interesting discussions, as you can imagine. You were certainly right that travel is an education.

That the father lived almost entirely by the stove is both good and bad. There was no getting near the heat—or the kitchen—without passing his lair. On the good side, he slept by his stove like a hibernating bear, leaving a bedroom, not much bigger than a closet, for Fritz and me. The bedroom floor was hard, my blanket—newly acquired from a secondhand stall—was thin and dirty and, yet, once the chair was hooked under the door handle—a precaution against, as Fritz puts it, *Papa wandering in the trenches*—I could honestly tell Nan that the room was *quite safe*.

Safer than the Adlon, I could honestly have written, for although my new lodging was in a seedy and unfashionable section of the city, it had the great advantage of not being near any of the establishments that now know all about Uncle Lastings. And me, too. Though I didn't want to worry Nan, I was on my way to being notorious.

This was a gradual process, you understand. Even though the criminal police were supposedly efficient, things were so quiet for so long that I thought Uncle Lastings had panicked unnecessarily. No one seemed concerned that some street-fighting, gun- or drug-dealing malcontent had been shot, a situation that suited me fine.

I hid out for a couple of days, keeping a watchful eye on the courtyard and on the tailor's shop and the secondhand furniture dealer that occupied the ground floor and getting to know Fritz's moody and dangerous parent. I saw few of the other tenants, some of whom departed for early jobs as I returned in the morning. The exception was Lisl, who lived three flights down. She was forever in the hall or the courtyard, playing with a ball or a jump rope—a thin, rickety-looking child with a great taste for chocolate, which I supplied in return for gossip about the rest of the building.

The little girl had a sharp, pinched face and knowing eyes. Just how knowing, I was soon to discover. Nightly we heard the sounds of the tango, the Charleston, and the Black Bottom issuing from her family's flat, which blossomed with pink-tinged lights at sundown and attracted a bevy of cabs and a good deal of foot traffic. There was laughter and shouts and sometimes applause. When I asked Lisl, she made a face and told me they put on shows.

Fritz was a little more forthcoming. The Schmitts were a bourgeois couple with two grown daughters, as well as Lisl and a handicapped son—a big blond lug with a cast in his eye. Owners of a shop that had gone under in the hyperinflation, they chose not to starve, as Fritz put it, and turned their front parlor into a venue for specialized sex shows: customer's choice. *They keep it in the family*, Fritz said. *Safer that way, don't you think? And there's no one else to pay.*

Uncle's *welcome circus of depravity*, indeed. I didn't feel that creative, so I gave Fritz the silver-mounted brushes to sell. He undoubtedly cheated me in the process, but we enjoyed some good dinners that cheered me up immensely. I kept the Leica in reserve, locked in my case. He surely knew I had it, and he would possibly filch it if he had a chance. I would in his place, so I could certainly add to my letter that *I am getting to know the real Berlin and the real Berliners.* Although not the worst part of the city, most residents of the district were a pretty sorry, shivering, underfed, and overworked lot. I wanted to avoid joining them.

And I had good prospects of doing so. Thanks to Fritz, I had my evening clothes and some makeup. As soon as I stopped seeing vengeful nationalists and suspicious coppers behind every lamppost, I sallied out to the clubs, where there was almost always a gentleman in need of company and in the possession of a comfortable hotel room. I can rough it on Fritz's floor if I have to, but I quite enjoy luxury. And if I stayed out all night, I could come back and collect Fritz's bed in the morning. The mattress was thin and dubious, of course, but better than the floor. I reckoned that I could survive in Berlin.

Things were going well, and I was thinking that I could put aside a little money, sell the Leica, and depart for London, when Fritz brought in a copy of *Arbeiter-Illustierte-Zeitung*, spread it out on his bed, and pointed to a story. I shook my head. While, thanks to his father, my grasp of *Deutsch* army profanity was improved, the narrow columns and Gothic script of the papers were still beyond me.

Fritz translated the headline: *More on the White Cat Murder.* And gave me a significant look. I tried to seem interested instead of alarmed.

The police today announced that they are seeking to question a young foreigner, English or American. The youth, aged probably 17 or 18, arrived at the bar much favored by right-wing fighters just before the incident last Tuesday night, when Hans Baasch, age 38, was murdered and his companion, Ernst Dittner, age 35, seriously wounded. The shooting occurred after what the bartender at the White Cat described as an argument between them and a tall, heavyset foreigner, probably British. The assailant is described as speaking fluent German and having a military bearing.

*No reason is known for the attack, but the shooting
occurred after the mysterious young man stopped at the bar.
Police believe that he signaled to the assailant in some way
because the shooting occurred immediately after he abruptly
left the establishment.*

*The man police wish to question is lightly built, 5'9" or
5'10", with dark brown hair and a fair complexion. He may
be related to the assailant, who operates under a number of
aliases, including Laurence Marsdon, and Luc Pinot.*

"Is maybe you, Francis?"

This was serious. I put on as bland a face as I could and said,
"Certainly not. And I've never heard my uncle called anything
but Lastings. He's a con man, not a killer. Most likely the man
they're looking for just stopped by for a drink."

Fritz gave me a look. His English has progressed by leaps and
bounds, and he anticipates a better job and useful connections
and maybe a chance to travel. He's ambitious, I've discovered,
and it crossed my mind that there might be a reward, that Fritz
might have omitted to read that information, that he might turn
me in. I started to tell him about Uncle Lastings, who was—and
I really did believe this at the time—about the last person in
Berlin to go around shooting rightists. "He runs the Society for
a Christian Europe for God's sake."

"As may be," said Fritz, "but much of Berlin is Red. Our
district, too, Father being the exception," he added under his
breath. "Whoever shot that reactionary militarist—a Freikorps
vet and now a National Socialist fanatic—would be welcome

here. He is, how you say"—he groped for words for a moment—
"a helper of the public?"

"Public benefactor," I said, and I thought how surprised
Uncle Lastings would be.

"Public benefactor," Fritz rolled the words around in his
mouth as if to taste them. He is clever, and he has not just a
talent but a love for languages. If I am not out for the night—
which I am fairly often, needing, as Uncle would say, *to replenish
the exchequer*—we sit on his bed. I read a Dickens novel aloud
to him, stopping whenever he does not understand a word or a
reference or when the verbs confuse him.

"Right," I said. "What were the names again, Marsdon and
Pinot? Whoever—he's no connection to me. Though," I added
when I saw he was still dubious, "it's admittedly a coincidence.
There could be some confusion." And some danger for me.

Fritz looked thoughtful. From then on, I was extra careful
to lock my suitcase before I went out for an evening. I kept a
close eye on the comings and goings in the seedy hallways and
in the dank and dirty courtyard below and bribed my little
friend Lisl with chocolates so that she would be alert for strangers as well.

Then the blow fell. Fritz was late coming back one evening,
and I was already dressed to go out. "Should we get a chop,
maybe? A bottle of wine before I head out?" I had been treating
us to decent meals nearly every night in an effort to keep him
firmly on my side.

"Not in that outfit," he said, and he shook his head.

"What's happened?"

He put his hand on my shoulder, and we sat down on his bed. "The police were at the hotel today."

"Well, I'm hardly surprised. Uncle Lastings must have run up a terribly big bill."

"They were many," Fritz said. "Plainclothes and some that did not smell like cop."

That did not sound good.

"There was a search of the room. The management is unhappy. Sealed rooms aren't useful."

"I can see that."

"I hung around the hallway. As if ready, if needed, you know." "And?"

"They were looking for something in the case."

"Well, we ate the silver brushes, but I did leave them a good pair of shoes and all Uncle's clothes. What cops need with gold cufflinks is beyond me, because even the whole lot couldn't have settled the bill."

Fritz shook his head and gave me a close look. "Maybe a camera?" he said.

"Why do you think that?"

"I heard them talking, *Kamera* and *Fotoapparat* and *Kamera-film*. Something they want badly."

"That camera will get me back to London. I'm keeping the camera."

"Has it film?" Fritz asked carefully.

"Haven't a clue. Not much good without it, though."

"I think they want that film," Fritz said. "And they think you have it."

"Why?"

"Questions about you. They want your suitcase. They would like to know how it left the hotel. If it left."

"Are you in trouble?" I asked, feeling guilty.

"I said you were always using stairs. This is—what is the word?"

"Eccentric."

"Yes, a good word. *Eccentric*. So the case could be on any floor. They will search." He shrugged. "Anyone could have found it. Taken it to the luggage storage. Guests do leave bags. Forget bags. A lot is possible."

That was an understatement.

"But, Francis, still there is trouble. We were all asked for descriptions. *Natürlich*, Albert gave a good one." He gave me a look. "What could I do?"

"Of course," I said. "And *last seen wearing a black dinner jacket?*"

"They will be looking in the clubs and the fancy cafés. And I think they will draw a picture. For the press."

A portrait! I would be famous. I felt rather sick. In this district, my name means nothing, but a picture would be both a danger and an inconvenience. To share Fritz's floor when I can be out and about most of the time was one thing. To be stuck in his flat day and night would be intolerable.

"I must leave here. You could come under suspicion."

"Yes," he said, crumpling the page and putting it beside the stove for the fire. "But people will not talk to the police here. Is good thing."

"A very good thing," I said and then added cautiously, "but could there be a reward?"

Fritz's face grew serious. "Nothing yet. That would be different. You are foreign, and we are poor."

Right. And my uncle, public benefactor though he might be, was an anti-Bolshevik working for the Society for a Christian Europe. I needed a new hiding hole.

CHAPTER FOUR

With only a couple of marks in my pocket, a final troll through the night cafés was in order, and while a police drawing could be disastrous, I reckoned I had a few more hours of safety and obscurity. I had long adjusted to danger. *I'm becoming a real cosmopolitan and nothing about Berlin fazes me now*, I wrote to Nan.

That was an exaggeration, but I no longer feared murderers lurking behind every door. I'd realized that I was nearly invisible in the street crowds and in the noisy, smoky pleasure palaces. Someone at a favorite boy bar or cabaret might recognize me, but I should be safe enough elsewhere, perhaps in a vaudeville crowd. Haller's or the Wintergarten were not Uncle Lastings's territory, and I'd only been to vaudeville once with Fritz, as I lack the German for the jokes and have no taste for either music or naked girls.

So, a vaudeville hall would be the ticket. I put on my evening clothes, made up my face—a difficult thing without a mirror and not nearly so much fun—and ventured out. I scraped up the entrance fee and paid for a good seat. Costumes, music, unintelligible comics—I took my cue from the crowd and laughed in the right places.

There were lots of young women wearing beads and feathers . . . when they weren't wearing sequins and chiffon. There were many old men with opera glasses and many young men who wished they'd brought some: all tedious. Even the famous Tiller Girls, they of the splendid legs and synchronized kicks, who Uncle Lastings would have called the *pièce de résistance*, didn't win me over. Polished as they were, I was mostly surprised to learn that they'd been imported all the way from London.

I didn't see anyone that I knew, but I'd miscalculated: The gentlemen seeking company were all focused on the stage, and if any of them had an eye for boys, they were taken with the strapping blond tenor or the sly master of ceremonies with his incomprehensible patter. Without a turn in my luck, I saw a dismal future as a *Schlafburschen*, which is quite as bad as it sounds and means someone who rents a bed for a few hours a day—or night. And not for fun, either. The worst of both worlds, so to speak.

I hung around the lobby and haunted the bar. Nothing doing. Having optimistically bought a decent dinner, I was too broke to swan into the cafés like a gentleman. Facing a long, dismal, and probably dangerous walk back to Fritz's, I was in as bad a mood as possible when I left with the last of the festive crowd. Their noise and laugher were so annoying that I turned into the alley that ran alongside the theater.

A fire escape took up virtually the breadth of the passage, and I was still within the shadow of its steps and supports when I heard an English voice, a London voice at that. I stopped. I hadn't been homesick until just that moment when my own language sounded unexpectedly sweet, even in anger, even shouted, even, as Nan would have said, *in a voice like a fishwife.*

It was coming from a woman, unusually tall and in unusually high heels, standing on the last step down from the stage door. She was slim and dark with short hair and a short dress and a chunky wrap, and she was trying to escape a large man in a homburg and a vicuña coat who had blocked her exit and who was threatening her—I could understand that much—in a low, harsh voice. She was having none of it, but she looked unsteady in her heels, and when he pulled his right hand out of his pocket and something glittered, I grabbed one of the support bars of the fire escape and swung out like Tarzan, yelling *Eaaaaaaw!* and connected with the man's back.

I hit him with both feet. He gave a sound between a bark and a deflating football and tumbled onto the asphalt with me on top of him.

"Blimey!" she cried and grabbed my hand. I found my feet, and we charged down the alley, my asthma making me wheeze and her high heels clattering on the paving. The woman began shouting, "*Taxi! Ein Taxi anhalten,*" before we reached the sidewalk. When an empty one appeared, she put two fingers in her mouth and whistled and shook her ruffled skirt to show off her remarkable legs.

The cab braked with a squeal, and, although there was a shout from the alley, she jumped in with me right behind her. "*Schnell,*

schnell!" she told the driver. We shot away from the curb as her assailant reached for the door.

She called out an address, then turned to say, "*Dankeschön*." I told her in English that she was welcome.

"My knight in shining armor." She gave me a close look and added, "Or is it in blusher and lipstick?"

"Mascara, too," I said, for I want my efforts appreciated. "But strictly for evening."

"Without a doubt, dearie," she said. "Moderation in all things, my old father used to say. Thank the Lord he never came to Berlin."

"It's for a certain taste," I said, for though I needed to leave, I was really not at all tired of the city.

"Give it time. The thing is," she added in a confidential manner, "one accumulates people here. And then one longs to be rid of them."

I knew just what she meant. Only mine at the moment were of a quasi-official nature.

"I'm Muriel, by the way."

I shook her hand. "Francis." No last names required.

"Where can we drop you, Francis?"

I hesitated. I wanted to spend as little time as possible at Fritz's. I particularly disliked returning in the night and passing his father's "sentry post." When disturbed, the old man was apt to reach for his bayonet, and while he was barely mobile without his crutches and his wooden foot, his reach was long enough to be alarming. There had already been a couple of incidents when Fritz had to convince him that it was not time to go *over the top*. He should have met my father.

"I'm rather at sixes and sevens at the moment."

"A Berlin malady. Need a place for the night?"

I nodded.

"I owe you. But no funny business."

"Furthest thing from my mind."

She laughed then and said, "You know how to flatter a girl. But it's all right, dearie. Enough excitement for one night." She tapped on the glass, and the cabbie drew up to an old stone building with shuttered windows.

Once inside, my curiosity got the better of me. "You must get a lot of hopeful blokes. After hours I mean."

"Stage-door johnnies. Worst type, though a girl I know found herself a baron—a penniless one. Here we go." She unlocked the second door down the hallway and switched on a light. The room was nearly as small as Fritz's, with a metal bed, a single chair, a sink, and a tiny counter with a one-burner stove. There was a strong odor of perfume, sausages, face powder, and mildew.

"No, I stay away from them; you should, too," she continued. "But Bruno's our dealer." She sniffed eloquently.

I must have looked surprised.

"You can't get through three numbers a night, a Saturday matinee, and morning rehearsals on beer and schnapps. Believe me, you can't."

"Did I make things worse?"

"This clever bloke I know told me that things naturally go from bad to worse. Law of physics, he told me, not that I would know. But no regrets, dearie. Bruno was out of line. I pay him regularly, even if I can't always pay him on time. He was thinking of a different arrangement," she said and added, "I'd sooner get a dose of the clap."

She took off her coat. "Loo's down the hall. Give me five minutes."

When I returned, she was smoking in bed. I was about to take the chair when she patted the quilt. "No use freezing. And without the lipstick you remind me of Will."

I took off my shoes and lay down beside her. "Will?"

"My brother. First Battle of the Somme," she said.

I leaned my head on her shoulder, which must have been the right thing to do, because Muriel talked quietly about her brother, whom she had loved, until I fell asleep.

She was up all too early the next morning, fiddling with coffee and doing some exercises that required a lot of thumping and stamping. "Rehearsal at eleven," she said, doing something complicated with her left leg. "You don't just jump out of bed and put your foot above your head. Have some coffee." She brought me a cup and sat down beside me with hers.

"You on the run?" she asked when we were reasonably caffeinated.

"Rather."

"Get out of Berlin."

I nodded.

"Do you have any money?"

"I've a camera I want to sell. A Leica."

"Worth something, but the street vendors will steal you blind. You take it to Mort, Mort Grünberg, the Jew who runs the pawnshop off the Alexanderplatz. Tell him Muriel sent you. He's a nice old fellow, and as honest as you'll get in the trade."

"You deal with him?"

"Just about every month. There's always something. I pawn my coat, gold bracelet, earrings—usual stage gypsy stuff. I redeem them when I get paid. Portable wealth is what you need in this racket," she said and patted my knee.

Good advice. That way if Uncle Lastings reemerged and wanted his camera, I could hand him the ticket.

Outside the flat, Muriel gave me a hug and hailed a cab. I walked to the tram stop and arrived back at Fritz's shortly before noon, intending to collect my things and head to the pawnbroker. I found his father up and out of his horse blanket. This was unusual and not necessarily a good sign. Although as disheveled and badly shaved as ever, the old man was fully dressed in a couple of thick sweaters as if expecting one of his rare visitors. But this time he had added an army greatcoat, worn and dirty enough to have seen the trenches, and he had his wooden foot on and his crutches at the ready. He was going out.

"I won't disturb you," I said, hoping he was well away from the western front at the moment. "I'm off for good." I put the key that Fritz used to hide for me on the table.

He stuck out one of his crutches to block my way. "You can't go now," he said, showing a lot of worn, yellowed teeth. "I've an appointment. You need to make yourself useful and watch the stove. See she doesn't overheat." He patted the stove as if it were a horse with a dubious temperament and gave me a malicious smile.

"All right." If he was going, I wanted him out of the way

promptly since I didn't figure to stick around one minute more than needed. I'd check the fire and leave as soon as I thought he'd be clear of the building.

He stumped to the door. "Keep an eye on it, lest you burn the place down," he said and, noisy with his crutches and his wooden foot, he made his way out. I changed my clothes and packed my bag. I hung the camera around my neck and went out to check the stove: hot but safely low on fuel.

Right! *Auf Wiedersehen!* to Fritz and crazy war vets. Bag in hand, I went to the door and turned the handle. Nothing. The old rascal had locked me in, and a glance at the table told me that he'd pocketed the extra key.

Damn! I kicked the table angrily and overturned a kitchen chair. That it was my own fault for leaving the key on the table only made me angrier. Herr Brotz could be out for an hour. He could be out for half a day. Seven flights down and up. Even if the old man walked better than I imagined, the stairs alone would be slow going, and delay could be fatal. Although as far as I could tell, there'd been nothing in any of the morning papers, I wouldn't put it past the enterprising *Mordkommission* to deliver my picture to the afternoon prints.

The big presses would already be churning out the afternoon news. Maybe with my photo. Maybe with a headline: *Wanted in Connection with the White Cat Murder.* Maybe with the information that there was a reward for one *Francis Bacon, 5'10", fair complexion, last seen wearing a black dinner jacket.* In my anxiety, billboard-size images of my face appeared on every street corner, and newsboys cried my name.

But there was nothing for it at the moment. As Nan says, *what can't be cured must be endured.* After a few moments of aimless panic, I began searching for something that might get the door open from the inside. I was beside the stove, poking through the old man's odds and ends, when I heard the key in the door.

Herr Brotz couldn't have gotten even as far as the ground floor. I straightened up warily, thinking that perhaps he had forgotten something. I was expecting him to stump in shouting about his things and nosy tenants but, no, it was not Fritz's father. Instead, two youngish men filled the doorway, both in dark jackets with soft workman's caps pulled down over their eyes. One carried a length of pipe. The other was large enough not to need anything except the massive paws that he now took out of his pockets, ready for action.

"*Guten Tag,*" I said, though my heart almost jumped out of my chest. "*Herr Brotz hier nicht.*" I tried unsuccessfully to smile. They were part of the crowd from the White Cat. I was sure of it.

The one with the pipe showed his teeth. "*Wo ist Herr Marsden?*"

"*Ich weiss nicht.*" I elaborated in my best mix of Deutsch and English that Herr Marsden—whom they must not discover was my uncle—had taken the *Zug* from the *Hauptbahnhof.* He was unreliable, he was gone, he was a dealer on the *Schwarzmarkt,* the black market. "*Ich weiss nicht,*" I repeated and stumbled into English to add that they were welcome to search the flat. It's amazing how a foreign vocabulary dissolves with nerves.

They looked at each other, and the big one nodded—body language I understood. They recognized me, I was sure of it, and they had come to do me damage. Heart thumping and gut contracting, I stepped back, brushed the top of the stove with my hand, and made contact with the bayonet belonging to Herr Brotz, previously Feldwebel Brotz of the western front.

The big man leaned casually against the door jam; clearly he didn't think he'd be needed. His partner took two steps into the room and raised the pipe. He had small, quick eyes and a nasty smirk—this wasn't work for him; this was pleasure.

Not for me. I was dreadfully frightened and angry, too, so I closed my hand around the bayonet with the sudden conviction that I would use it. I edged away from the entangling horse blanket and the various bits and bobs of Brotz Senior, keeping the chair between us so that they would not see the bayonet.

Could I avoid the man with the pipe? Could I somehow manage the hall? Or was my best hope to run into the bedroom and try to barricade the door? Indecisive, I made a feint toward the door, and the man swung the pipe at my head. I jerked back, the pipe landed against the padding of the chair, and, terrified, I thrust at his arm, which instantly opened red. He gave a yelp and dropped the pipe. Shoving the chair aside, I lunged forward, frantic to reach the hall and the stairs. The bigger man was blocking the way, but he was slow to react. Clutching the bayonet in both hands, I drove it through his jacket and into his side, just like the soldiers I had seen practicing so long ago at their base near the Curragh.

He gave a terrible cry and fell back into the hallway, ripping the weapon from my hands. I leaped past him and raced down the stairs, risking a fall at every step, pivoting around the banister posts at each landing. I heard Herr Brotz's voice a floor down, but whatever he shouted was lost in the clatter of my feet and in the shouts above. *Keep going, keep going*, I told myself. By the fourth floor, I was beginning to stumble, and I paused for a moment, grasping the railing and willing my protesting lungs to calm down.

On to the third, the second. I risked a glance above, but there was no one on the stairs. The bayonet had been razor sharp, and they had plenty to deal with. I stopped to catch my breath, which was momentarily threatening a permanent departure, when a door opened. I was at Lisl's flat, and the child was standing wide-eyed in the doorway. I gestured to warn her, but she held the door open and beckoned.

I shook my head and waved her away.

"*Es einen Mann außerhalb,*" she said and rattled on in great excitement. Out of all the verbiage, I understood *einen Mann*. The nosey little thing had spotted another man outside, who was waiting in case the victim escaped, with or without the help of a fine Prussian weapon. That was always their way, she said, and I believed her.

Lisl pulled me into the apartment and bolted the heavy door, then led me to the window. Through the heavy net curtain, I saw a man pacing back and forth before the main door. I couldn't see his face, only the top of his soft cap and the plume of smoke from his cigarette. "*Ja?*" Lisl said.

"*Ja.*" I sat down heavily on the floor, and it was a few minutes before I could get back onto my feet. "*Danke,*" I said and apologized for not having any chocolate.

She gave an unsettling smile and said that I could help her instead.

"*Gute*," I said, but I didn't want to make trouble for her family.

"Those men won't come here." She rubbed her fingers together in the universal sign for money. "Papa explains," she said and, with that, she led me into a back room and told me to wait.

CHAPTER FIVE

Noises in the hall. Someone rattled doorknobs in the corridor then ran up the stairs. A heavy tread—boots were much favored by the quasi-military fighters. The apartment building fell silent again; most of the residents were at work or nursing their sorrows elsewhere. Then, several minutes later, more commotion with a great deal of profane German, some of it new to me. The wounded combatants were being helped down the stairs, and I was relieved. They couldn't be too badly hurt. Understand that I had no regrets, but I was already of interest to the police, and the business with the bayonet probably qualified as an "assault with a deadly weapon."

More noise. The shuffling, stumbling, dragging of wounded limbs, past the second floor and down to the bleak lobby. Lisl ran in and called me to the window. Through the lacy mesh of the curtain, I saw three men: the two who had attacked me and their sentry. One had his arm wrapped up in what looked like a shirt. The other was bent over like a man of seventy, clutching his side. Their uninjured companion set off at a trot, returning a few minutes later with a cab, and helped the other two inside.

Lisl nodded and gave me a quick, sly grin. They were bad men, she told me. I agreed and thought that it was time to leave. Although I could kiss my dinner jacket and my collection of gallery catalogues good-bye, I had escaped two homicidal thugs. I also had my leather jacket, thirty pfennigs, and the Leica. With luck, I'd get out of Germany, and I was about to wish her *auf Wiedersehen* when Lisl pulled me back from the window.

The cab was driving away with my two assailants, but their sentry was still on duty, and he had turned to scan the building. There was only one exit, and he knew it. Would he come looking upstairs? Even if he didn't, I couldn't leave, not under his nose. I was frightened, imagining pictures of the mysterious Herr Bacon in every paper, as well as alert coppers, tattletale citizens, and my probable arrest and eventual detention in some ghastly Prussian institution.

It took me a few minutes to remember what Nan used to say when I was carrying on about something: *You're not the only pebble on the beach, Francis.* How important was I after all? Possibly there was no drawing or a very poor one or even a good one that might pass unnoticed. I was overreacting. If I could remain for a few hours at the Schmitt's, I could use the dark to make my exit.

That was the plan I unfolded to Herr Schmitt, Lisl's papa, who arrived in time for supper with the rest of the family. At first glance—and at second glance, too—the Schmitts were a typical bourgeois family. Shabby but genteel dress, mended coats, and polished but well-worn shoes. Frau Schmitt was a blowsy blonde with a red face and a stout figure. She had small blue eyes with white eyelashes and a pursed red mouth.

The girls, no older than I, were slimmer versions of their

mother. Both wore short dresses and high-laced boots. They had stiff, nearly white bleached hair, and smooth, hard faces that suggested they could take care of themselves. Their brother, Klaus, was another matter. Big, over six feet, and broad with enormous hands and feet, he had a vague, puzzled expression and a slack red mouth. He carried a tiny toy truck in one hand, and he was humming softly to himself.

Lisl got out a big iron pan and began frying sausages and onions and heating sauerkraut, and her papa laid a loaf of bread on the table, arousing hopes of dinner. Lisl introduced me with much excitement, and her parents exchanged glances. Then Herr Schmitt signaled for me to follow him into the back room. He was not at all what I expected, with a thin, dry face and graying hair. His eyes were light hazel, much enlarged by his thick glasses. He looked more like an accountant than the impresario of a sex show. He spoke clear, if careful, English.

He demanded an account, and I told him that two men had broken into Herr Brotz's. Thieves, I thought. I was attacked but, fortunately, I'd remembered Herr Brotz's souvenir bayonet. There were injuries—not too severe, I assured him—but one of their colleagues was still lurking below. I added that as I was leaving Berlin as soon as possible, and I would prefer not like to involve the police.

Then I waited while Herr Schmitt thought things over, a process that took some time. I was almost ready to take my chances on the street or—maybe equally daring—to return to Fritz's flat, when he said, "I know the man outside. A bad type, ex-Freikorps. Possibly you were mistaken for someone else."

"I hadn't thought of that," I said, as though this new idea was both plausible and reassuring. "But I don't want to bring trouble." Actually, except for Lisl, I wouldn't have worried for a minute.

"Oh, you are safe here." His tone was smug. "The police take an interest in our little operation."

He must have seen my alarm, because he added, "We attract steady clients as well as the tourists. All very safe because *alle in der Familie*." He pronounced their business motto with satisfaction. "The police appreciate that. Conducive to good order. Good order, good fun—that's our aim."

I had a sudden appreciation of what Uncle Lastings called being *down the rabbit hole*. "If I could stay, please, until I can leave safely . . ." I said and added, in case he expected money, "Unfortunately, most of what I own is still in Herr Brotz's flat."

"Do not think of going there!" he said. "Brotz is in with a bunch of Freikorps vets. Not that we reject any contribution."

I pulled out my thirty pfennings. "Otherwise my pockets are empty."

He waved away this trifle. "No matter. We have a special tonight, and Lisl dislikes working with Klaus. He is a sweet boy, but acting is hard for him."

I could imagine that, and other quite disgusting things. I couldn't help saying, "Lisl is maybe—ten?"

"Twelve. Old enough." His eyes were chilly. "She was never hungry, though in this very building some starved to death. But Klaus is big, and she is small. You"—he gave me a speculative look—"maybe are not so interested in women?"

I allowed this.

"Perfect. Stay and eat with us, and I can explain this evening's program. Something artistic," he said, with creepy enthusiasm. "I think you will—how do you say—do extra good?"

"Excel?"

"*Ja*, I think you will excel in the role."

The prospect of my theatrical debut almost, but not quite, took away my appetite.

After supper, the Schmitts cleared a space in their front room, moved in a metal bed with a collection of pillows, and arranged an assortment of chairs to form a little theater. The heavy curtains were closed, a selection of gramophone records organized, and some quite elaborate lighting readied. "So important for the mood," Herr Schmitt told me.

Mine wasn't very good, despite a supper of sausages, bread, and kraut. If the sentry hadn't persisted in lurking below, I'd have made my escape, even though I wouldn't have to do anything complicated. But as this was a command performance, Herr Schmitt let me know that my part was crucial. He was depending on me, he said, and he actually spoke of "taste and discretion," which normally would have driven me to some excess.

Lisl was a different matter. She had her hair in two braids so that she looked like a child of eight. She was dressed in a pinafore with crotchless lace bloomers underneath, white stockings, and black patent leather child's shoes. There was something for every appetite in Berlin, but this one left a bad taste. Still, Lisl was depending on me, and she came and put one small hand on my knee and looked into my eyes.

There is no fairness in life. I am thirsty for sensation, the stronger the better most times, and I only occasionally get what

I want. She was the opposite. She'd experienced too much, I guessed, and wanted to feel less. Or nothing. I nodded to her and pointed to her lipstick.

She produced a tube from the pocket of her pinafore, a ridiculous garment that reminded me of my sisters' dresses. I picked up the dog whip and ran the lipstick along the one side. I slapped the untouched side on my hand, then turned the whip over and slapped with the other side. A fine red line ran across my palm. "*Ja?*"

"*Sehr gute!*"

So I was into the spirit of the thing, and we were ready. I sat down on the only seat left, a sagging hassock, and Lisl sat on my lap as if this were the most natural thing in the world. Around us, her sisters were squeezing into peculiar corsets, and Frau Schmitt, already attired in a fluttery negligee, was finishing up with a spritz of perfume and clouds of powder.

Out front, the patrons—Herr Schmitt called them "our honored guests"—were arriving. The gramophone was playing some noisy syncopation, and the red shaded lamps were casting what now seemed to me a sinister glow, especially since at least one audience member was in military dress and another was clearly police. Fortunately, Herr Schmitt, set to perform with his wife after a "Lesbian Interlude" with the two girls, produced a mask for me.

"Special request," he said. He was flushed, and without his glasses, I could see that his eyes were dilated, no doubt with the ubiquitous white powder of the Berlin night. He said, "A good time to be had by all."

He waited until I put on the mask and pronounced himself satisfied. "Not so young now."

Fine. I felt like twelve again and ready to step out for some hor-rid school play, but in moments I would impersonate a lecherous schoolmaster eager to strip and then beat Lisl—bruises optional but blood highly desirable. Hence the lipstick. I put a second coat on the dog whip and put the tube in my pocket as a reserve.

Making noises out front, Frau Schmitt was doing her best to enhance her husband's efforts. It was what Nan would have called *a fine to-do*. You bet. Meanwhile, I struggled to keep from wheezing amid the musk and powder of the "dressing room" and the cigar smoke creeping in from the audience. At last, applause. Frau Schmitt appeared wrapped in a sheet with Herr Schmitt behind her, belting a red velvet dressing gown. He had hairy legs and a hairy white chest.

"*Schnell, schnell,*" he said and waved us out front for the com-mand performance—the highlight of the evening, the cost of my escape.

I put on the mask, scratchy with buckram and glue. Lisl took my hand, and I stumbled after her, unable to see clearly behind the eyeholes. Fortunately, my dialogue was minimal, and I remembered it, announcing in intelligible German that it was time for her lesson. I turned to the assembled and rubbed my hands together like a villain in a kino.

A ripple of excitement in response.

"*Nein,*" said Lisl. Her voice was appropriately pathetic.

"*Ja,*" said the schoolmaster, who grabbed her and set her on his knee. The lesson went downhill from there, and Lisl wound up pantaloon-free and face-down, being lambasted with the dog whip. Shades of my father, who had favored just such correction for me. The whole thing was bad, disgusting really, and the last thing in the world I'd ever want to do sexually.

Still, credit where it's due, I was pretty skillful. Without a drop of real blood in sight, Lisl's back and bottom were soon a mesh of red slashes, an illusion promoted by her shrieks and pleas. She was so realistic that more than once I pulled my arm back in alarm, only to get a good pinch on the leg from my "victim." She was a trooper—or more likely and depressingly—frightened of failure.

Finally, various groans and gasps in the audience signaled satisfaction. I released my grasp, and Lisl bolted, half-naked, out of the room. I stood up, made a proper Prussian bow as instructed (a key thing according to Herr Schmitt) and followed her into the "dressing room," where her father poured us each a small glass of schnapps and Frau Schmitt took a towel and began cleaning Lisl's back. All in the family, indeed.

I couldn't wait to get out of there, but for safety's sake I had to swallow the Schmitts' compliments—many and fulsome—and their hints that I might be employed as an honorary member of the tribe. More agreeably, Herr Schmitt gave me twenty marks, which in the city counted as decent money. I lay on the floor of the children's room, wide awake with Klaus snoring and snuffling and Lisl talking in her sleep, until near dawn, when I crept through to the front room, full of a stale and disagreeable stink, and checked the window. The sidewalk was empty. The sentry did not reappear once the sun came up.

I hung the Leica over my shoulder, thanked the Schmitts, kissed Lisl's cheek, and set out to escape Berlin.

CHAPTER SIX

With my new wealth, I rode to the Alexanderplatz, crowded with buses and trams and busy with street work. Gaping holes in the road, pipes on the sidewalks, and boardwalks, noisy with pedestrian clatter, over newly made ditches. On every corner, men with picks and shovels were removing concrete and tarmac and loading earth into wheelbarrows to trundle to the waiting horse carts. I spent a quarter of an hour amid obstacles and detours before I spotted the Grünberg pawnshop. On the lowest floor of a massive soot-blackened apartment building, it was a low, dark store with an assortment of goods in the window: clothes, musical instruments, pots and pans, carpenter's tools, a handsome armchair—a sad mix of modest luxuries and dire necessities.

A bell jangled as I went in, and the tiny, white-haired man with thick glasses and a green clerk's eyeshade straightened up from his high stool behind the counter. He looked dry and fragile and very old.

"*Guten Morgen*," I said and laid the camera case on the counter. "Do you handle cameras?"

"I deal with everything but food and livestock." His English was heavily accented but fluent. He took the Leica out of its case and turned it over in his hands carefully. "This is a fine camera, nearly new." He gave me a questioning glance, his eyes sharp. I had no doubt he had already valued the Leica to the penny and made a guess as to how much—or how little—I would take.

"It was my . . . late uncle's." I realized that, scruffy as I was, I must have looked dubious and added, "He died very suddenly as we were traveling together. Now I need money to get home." Did that sound right? I probably should have said "to ship his body home" like a devoted nephew. But with Uncle Lastings on the run and probably as lively as ever, I wasn't too concerned with his supposed corpse.

"My condolences," he said.

I thanked him. "My sole inheritance." I nodded toward the camera.

He scribbled some figures on a slip of paper. "One hundred and fifty marks," he said with an eloquent shrug. "Is worth more, but few can afford to buy such things today."

I was pleasantly surprised, and a little puzzled that my uncle, who had not been interested in the tourist sights and who hadn't taken a single picture that I knew of, should have had such a valuable camera.

The pawnbroker wrote out a ticket and told me not to lose it. "No ticket, no camera," he said. "Remember whoever holds the ticket gets the item."

I nodded.

"*Sehr gut*. No other way to do business." He went to his cash drawer and counted out the marks. Enough, I was sure, to get me out of Germany. I put the cash and the ticket into my wallet, and I was turning to leave when he said, "You are forgetting the film."

So I had. "I don't know what I'd do with it," I said.

"Perhaps there are some souvenir photos you might like." He turned a knob, opened the camera, and handed me the film cassette. "There is a camera shop on the next block that will develop the pictures for you."

And what might they be? Boys cheap and pretty? Portly widows with good bank accounts? Or some other enthusiasm? I wasn't interested, but to be polite, I stuck the cartridge in my pocket and forgot about it. I was leaving Berlin, and I was excited to go. From one of the street vendors, I bought a second-hand knapsack, a shirt, some socks, and a soft workman's cap—a lame idea of a disguise as it turned out—and hurried to the main station.

At the big board of arrivals and departures, I studied the cities: Vienna, Brussels, Warsaw, Prague, Budapest. Leaving Ireland to live alone in London had been a great adventure, but here was all the world with connections via Hamburg to New York and even Buenos Aires. The letters and numbers on the board rattled and reassembled every few seconds as trains arrived at the various platforms. Where to go? What to see?

Everything seemed so enticing that it was a few minutes before I remembered my situation. The romance of travel was fine and good, but I'd be safer back on British soil. What I needed was a through train connecting via the Channel ferry all the way to Victoria Station and available for boarding within the hour. I settled for a second-class seat to Cologne, leaving in twenty minutes. With a little luck, I could make my way from there in stages, as I reckoned I was too insignificant to attract interest outside Berlin.

I took my seat. Across from me were two nuns in their black habits and what I recognized as a sporting type with plus fours, red whiskers, and a discontented expression. Should I give him the eye as a possible source of financial support? I thought not. He was more likely a turf accountant who'd taken a loss at the recent meeting. I knew those types from my father. I nodded to him and smiled at the nuns.

We were soon joined by a thin and anxious-looking young woman in a worn coat with a black mourning band on the arm. She came equipped with a suitcase so enormous that it took both me and Whiskers to put it onto the rack for her. She thanked us and slumped in the seat, eyes streaming, and sniffled into her handkerchief.

Nuns and a mourner were hardly good omens, especially since the weeping lady was doused in a rose-scented perfume that set my nose itching. The final passenger for our compartment arrived after we had pulled away from the station. He rattled the door open and, swaying with the accelerating train, stepped inside. He was fair and exceptionally tall with a lot of curly hair, and he was wearing a fine English pinstriped suit. When he wished us *Guten Tag*, I heard his accent. Fancy businessman? Something with our embassy? A well-heeled tourist traveling for his health? All possible. If I hadn't been so excited about traveling and so nervous about being stopped, I'd have asked myself what he was doing in second class with his fancy suit and expensive shoes.

He dropped into the seat beside me, put his attaché case on the floor between his feet, and straightened his jacket with very white, very well-kept hands. "Stopping at Cologne?" he asked me after a few minutes.

"Not for long."

"Make time to see the Dom; the cathedral is famous."

I said I would and wondered if I might be lucky. He looked like money, and he looked interested. I stood up, collected my knapsack, and went to change my filthy shirt in the loo. I washed my face, combed my hair as best I could, then stood at the window out in the corridor, enjoying some air and making myself available for a private chat. I watched the ticket taker approaching from the next car. When he arrived, brisk and official, he punched my ticket without giving me a second glance, a minor triumph.

I'd purchased a ticket. I'd gotten it punched. I was safe, I thought, until the border, where my passport would be examined. Tricky to be sure, but my success thus far gave me confidence. With my knapsack slung over my shoulder, I leaned against the wall and watched the flat countryside roll by. When the man in the pinstriped suit emerged from our compartment to stand beside me, I was able to give him a friendly, casual smile.

"Don't look around," he said in a low voice. "Just follow me."

All right!

Through our carriage and through the next two. I had visions of a late lunch, of beer and schnapps—or better, some pale

German wine. But my companion had other ideas. He stopped at the exit steps of the car. "The train reaches the first station in two minutes. We get off then."

High romance but no thank you. "I've a ticket to Cologne," I said. "I fancy seeing that cathedral you recommended."

"Take my advice or what you'll see is the inside of a Prussian reform school—if you're lucky. There are two plainclothes Kripos right behind us with that railway policeman."

My stomach dropped and rebounded into the back of my throat. "What of it?" I said as boldly as I could manage. "They're nothing to me."

"Oh, but they will be, Herr Bacon." He knew my name, and that alone gave him credibility. I looked back through the doors to the next compartment and caught a glimpse of the high-peaked cap of a railroad cop. My would-be rescuer in the fancy suit might be telling the truth. When the train slowed down with wheezing brakes and a rush of steam, he opened the exit door and I jumped down after him. We stepped onto the plat-form, half-stumbling, half-running, and made it to the stairs and down to the street before we could be followed. Partway along the block, he indicated a dark saloon car and a bulky red-faced driver who reminded me of some of my father's squad. Ex-military, I guessed.

My acquaintance from the train was something else, and when he ordered me into the car, I hesitated. I wanted to know who he was and where he was from, but he produced a revolver from his elegant case. It wasn't nearly as impressive as Uncle Last-ings's Webley, but it was awfully close to me, and I obeyed.

"Where are we going?" I asked as we pulled away from the curb. "You've cost me a ticket to Cologne."

"Your wallet, please," he said in reply.

I fished it out of my pocket.

"Your uncle left you with a bit of cash, I see." He turned over my remaining marks.

"My uncle left me broke." I realized instantly I'd been foolish to tell him anything.

"But you are nothing if not resourceful," he remarked. "Eluding the police, obtaining funds for a journey. A young man of parts, as they used to say. Ah," he said, lifting the pawn ticket. "Grünberg's, the pawnshop of choice. Let me guess. A new Leica?"

He had the ticket; there was no point in lying. I nodded. He put the pawn ticket into his own wallet and returned mine with the cash. "To the Alexanderplatz," he told the driver.

"So who are you?" I asked.

"You can call me Harold, and I've just saved you from arrest."

"So you say."

"Show him, Mac."

The driver picked up the newspaper on the front seat and passed it back. It was folded to an interior page with a police drawing and the headline, *Youth Sought in White Cat Shooting*. I could just about translate the first line of the story: *Criminal police wish to question English tourist, Francis Bacon, age 17, about the recent murder of . . .*

"It's not a very good likeness," I said, although I knew that didn't matter. The Germans liked paperwork. They enjoyed demanding one's papers, recording one's name, checking one's passport. I'd met any number of nice boys who lacked the right documents and had to keep a weather eye out for the police.

"So if you want to see London again anytime soon, you'll be a good boy and do what I tell you."

I wondered if he was propositioning me, but even that idea did not cheer me up. I slumped back in the seat and said nothing. It was entirely possible that my next letter would begin, *Dear Nan, I am writing you from a Prussian reformatory. Please don't worry too much, but thanks to Uncle Lastings, I have been charged with murder. . . .*

An exaggeration, Francis; Nan used to warn me of that. I think the real charge would be *accessory before the fact.* I know that, thanks to Nan. Because she is a great fan of murder cases, both real and fictional, I did not need Harold to tell me that I was in serious trouble.

He read the paper on the drive back to Berlin, throwing out occasional comments, which I ignored. Near the Alexanderplatz, we were caught in the confusion of street work, pedestrians, horse carts, and trams. It was slow going, and when our driver cut off one of the trucks, we got a burst of angry German from its driver and shouts from the gang of men in the back. One word rang a bell: *diplomat.* How would they know that? The car must have diplomatic plates. I was in the hands of His Majesty's government.

Was that a cause for celebration—or alarm? Anyone born in Ireland must have doubts.

Harold gave the street address for Grünberg's, and his driver squeezed the big car between the tram tracks and the construction and into the side street for the pawnshop. The pavement was narrow, and there were some mounds of earth that almost blocked the sidewalk.

Would he of the pistol and the fine suit really help me? Could he get me out of Germany? Would he? The Leica, I realized, had been my only card, and as I leaned back against the seat miserably, I saw nothing else that made me valuable. My nose began to itch as it did sometimes when I was anxious and my asthma was thinking of kicking up. I reached for my handkerchief and touched the film cassette in my jacket pocket.

Of course! Thank you, Herr Grünberg! In that instant, I threw off despair and struggled to keep from smiling. Surely it wasn't the camera Harold wanted. Even a new Leica was not valuable enough to send a diplomat jumping from trains and waving a pistol.

For some inconceivable reason, he must want the film. But if I gave it to him, my usefulness would be at an end, and my chest tightened up at the thought. What then? Nothing good. By the time Mac found a place to idle the car, I had made up my mind. Harold got out, warning me to stay where I was. I waited until Grünberg's door closed behind him, then unlocked my side and dived into the street.

Mac gave a shout, but I ran into the path of a cyclist with a big market basket, causing him to brake to avoid the open door of the saloon car. Around the piles of earth, past a vendor selling lengths of cloth, down the first alley, and back onto the main *Platz*, where an incoming tram was slowing. I hopped onto the back platform and pushed forward to grab a seat.

I changed trams twice and got out in an unfamiliar working-class district, where I loitered away the afternoon at a boy bar. It was dingy but warm with a coal stove and seemed as much a clubhouse as a watering hole. Promising customers were apparently few and far between, for the boys were playing cards and gossiping over glasses of Schultheiss-Patzenhofer and the fumes of the inevitable Salem Aleikum cigarettes.

As scruffy as I looked, I didn't get a second glance. Perhaps just as well; I still didn't know if there would be money in turning me in. I drank a couple of beers and worried about my situation. I had something Harold wanted, and he had the very thing I needed—an exit from Deutschland. We could do a swap, if only I had a safe way to meet him—not the easiest thing when I had little money and bad papers. With my face in the news, the popular cafés were going to be a danger. And while quiet and deserted places might be safer in one way, they would leave me at the mercy of Harold's revolver and the capable and muscular Mac.

No, I had to meet him somewhere public, preferably respectable, and count on an English dislike of making a scene to keep me safe. I tried to plan without much success, until I realized I could understand snatches of the conversation at the next table. One boy was complaining with eloquent gestures that his best girl, one Erika—of an abundant superstructure and spectacular legs—was crazy about clothes.

Not normally an interest of mine, but at that moment a light went on. Thank you, Erika, whoever you may be. That night, quite late, I made my way back to the alley beside the vaudeville hall to wait for my friend Muriel, the dancer.

CHAPTER SEVEN

A clatter of heels on the steps—one, two, three tall women with feathers in their hats and smart coats. "Toodle-oo!" one called, and they tripped away laughing. Could I have come too late? Could I have missed Muriel?

The door opened again, and there she was, a vaudeville goddess, tall and handsome, wrapped in a fox stole. "I see someone's made a killing," I said.

"Francis! You like?" She did a pirouette. "He's short, ugly, and rich. Quite the man of my dreams. But fancy seeing you here!"

"I'm back like a bad penny. I need your help, Muriel."

She gave me a close look. "Your makeup certainly isn't all it could be."

I took her arm as we started toward the main street. "I'll pay for the cab," I offered.

She stopped. "You're in real trouble?"

"I have a way to get out of it."

"Dearie, I've heard that one before." She sounded so skeptical I was afraid she was going to tell me to get lost. But maybe her new fur had put her in a good mood, or maybe she thought I'd brought her luck, because once I unfolded my plan, she broke out laughing.

"You kill me, Francis. You really do."

"I can pay," I said, "and if all goes well, I'll return the dress. Dry cleaning, too," I added in desperation.

"Listen, you gave me a laugh. I should have an old frock you can wear, but you'll need a coat."

"I'm tough," I said. "Get me a dress and a pair of shoes I can walk in, and I'll stand the cold."

Muriel laughed again, patted me on the shoulder, and said, "It might be easier to go for a soldier."

That was not likely. We took a cab together, and I slept squeezed on one side of her narrow bed. She had me up in good time the next morning, and when Muriel mentioned that she could use her landlady's phone, I persuaded her to call the consulate and ask for Harold.

"There really is such a person," she said when she came back upstairs—how could she have doubted me? "He will meet you at the Romanisches Café at one o'clock. There were threats," she added. "He is not a nice man."

I apologized for Harold, although he was hardly my responsibility, and Muriel went to her closet for a maroon frock. Not a color I'd have chosen, but it was loosely cut and it fit well enough that she became enthusiastic about the project. She sacrificed a short coat to the overall effect, although she balked at a pair of stockings, which I thought was rather a shame. I had to be content with a black line up the back of each leg to suggest a seam.

Shoes had been my biggest concern, but dancers have large feet and a rather shabby pair of hers was just stretched enough to be possible. "You'll be sitting most of the time," Muriel said.

"Right." The shoes were ankle-bending, heel-torturing devices, but they gave me an extra few inches that I quite fancied.

After Muriel was sure I could walk without stumbling, she got out her makeup and some hair pomade and went to work. I got my eyes done and lipstick and a good deal of rouge and powder. She put a few curls in my hair, and when she worried that my coiffeur was too short to be plausible, she found a cloche that, yes, made me look ready to dance the Charleston. I took a look in her mirror. "You're a genius," I said.

"An anonymous one, remember."

I kissed her hand and promised. She had a paper sack from Wertheim's, and I put my own shoes and clothes into it. "I'll look as if I've been shopping," I said. "Yes?"

"Yes, indeed. But less with the hips, dearie. You don't want to scare him off."

I didn't think Harold scared easily, but she was right, less was more. I wanted to look like a real Berlin girl—neat and anonymous, not one of the over-the-top queens from the Eldorado. I walked carefully, smaller steps, shoulders still, down to the tram stop. By the time I got out at the Kaiser Wilhelm Memorial Church and crossed to the Romanesque pile that housed the café, I felt pretty confident. I could certainly walk, although I wouldn't want to run. I hadn't raised any eyebrows, either, though one nice chap had offered me his seat.

The church clock struck the hour as I made my way past the

sparsely occupied outside tables. Have I mentioned my father's fetish with punctuality? Useful on this occasion, and I went bang on time into the café, an exciting place I'd visited with Uncle Lastings. The Romanisches was the intellectuals' hangout, full of feuding artists arguing styles to the death over beer and schnitzel.

But no art today! I hesitated at the door of the first room and looked around. There was no sign of Harold, but several men smiled at me as I passed their tables, and I gave my hips a twitch. Muriel really was clever. I finally spotted my man in an alcove at the back, well away from the high, bright windows.

I sashayed up to him, set my shopping bag on a chair and said, "*Guten Tag, mein Herr.*"

He looked up with a kind of panicky annoyance and flapped his hand to indicate dismissal. I'd always imagined diplomats as suave and ready for any eventuality.

"No points for being on time?" I asked and sat down.

His face was a picture, as Nan would say, and it took him a few seconds to rearrange his expression.

"An unexpected getup, but I want to make it home in one piece."

Harold coughed and seemed to recover. He waved to the waiter, ordered a beer, and asked what the *Fräulein* would have. I gave a coy smile and asked for champagne. I deserved it, as my feet were already beginning to ache. How Muriel danced in these things was beyond me.

Harold waited until our drinks were on the table, then he leaned forward, touched my glass with his, and whispered, "Do you have the film?"

"Grünberg took it out when I left the camera. I'd forgotten all about it."

"An expensive omission," Harold said sourly.

"Costing me a ticket to Cologne," I reminded him.

He held out his hand. "I want that film."

"And I want to leave Germany. I want papers to get me over the border. And to keep me safe here in the meantime."

Harold looked down his nose and took an official tone. "We cannot interfere with German police business. The republic has its own system of justice."

This was bad. If he was unwilling to make a deal, I would be in the soup. Maybe I already was, because, with a little twinge of fear, I remembered Harold's driver. Could he be lurking outside? Ready to follow me? Ready to apply some ghastly combat skill? *Put the best face on it, Francis*, Nan used to say. "That's too bad," I said. "The film will be lost forever."

He grabbed my arm, but I didn't budge. I was right; he didn't want a scene. I'd only taken a sip of my champagne, so the glass was almost full. I held the little cartridge over the wine. "Ruin it if it goes in, I think." With my best flirtatious smile, I put the film back into my coat pocket.

Harold studied me for a moment before he produced an identity card with my face on it. He'd had it the whole time and had hoped to get the film without handing it over, which I thought was rather a mean trick. The identity card described me as an art student, which gave me a funny little twinge, and claimed my name was Francis Wood.

"This is no good. I'll need a passport."

"Passports take time. For the moment, you need papers. When you register, inform the police that your passport was stolen and that the embassy has issued you a temporary document. Naturally, you will not go in any such outlandish outfit."

I thought that unkind, considering he had been fooled, but I nodded. Although I was fond of lace underwear and silk stockings, I didn't fancy even another hour in Muriel's shoes.

"Also," he held out his hand, "your present passport—should you be found with it, there would be unpleasant questions."

Moment of truth. Could I trust Harold? I was quite sure I could not. Had I another option? Not at the moment. And I was certainly better off with a good document than with the papers of an *accessory before the fact*. I put the card in my pocket, handed over the film and my passport, and took a big drink of champagne.

"We will see what is on the film," Harold said. Now that he had the cartridge, there was a definite change in atmosphere. "We may be in touch in case you have contact with your uncle."

"What does my uncle do?"

Harold flapped his hand. Now he was a Man of Secrets. No doubt on a Mysterious Errand.

He stood up, put money on the table, and, to my surprise, held out his arm. "We leave together," he said sourly. "It would look odd otherwise after champagne."

Which had been excellent, even though I had been too nervous to enjoy it. I hoped it had put a hole in his budget. We walked through the café to the nods and bows of the waiters, so elegant in their dark suits and white aprons. Out past the exterior tables with the scavenging pigeons underfoot. Along the sidewalk. Was Harold continuing to escort me farther than was really necessary? Did he have other plans for me? As we started across the street, I looked left and right for a dark saloon car with diplomatic plates and a military chauffeur.

What I saw instead was a motorcycle that swung out behind an oncoming tram, cut back in front, bounced over the rails, and swerved directly toward us. I jerked my arm from Harold's grasp, pushed him clear and, unsteady in Muriel's heels, tumbled after him as the bike roared by with a sudden, sharp explosion that rattled against the rails. Then came the great wheeze of tram brakes, and a metallic screech as parts of the motorbike scraped against the curb. There was a clatter and a shot—it was clearly a shot—before the grinding acceleration of the bike rose over the confusion and whined away into the distance.

I scrambled dizzily to my feet within a couple of yards of the stalled tram, caught one of Muriel's shoes in the track, and snapped off the heel. My left side felt as if it had been crushed, and the unevenness of the shoes meant every hobbling step was painful. Across the tram tracks, Harold had gotten onto his knees, but from the red oozing over the front of his jacket, he wasn't going to get much farther. People were rushing out of the cafés and crowding nearer, calling for the *Polizei*, which might be disastrous, and for the *Krankenauto*, which I guessed we both needed.

Fortunately, Mac had already pushed his way through the crowd to seize Harold. Though the diplomat was much the larger man, Mac got him to his feet, caught him under the arms, and hustled him toward the same dark car that had brought me back to Berlin. I kicked off both my shoes and followed them. Mac wasn't keen to let me in the car, but Harold, white-faced and in obvious pain, flapped his hand and said, *"Schnell, schnell, Fräulein."*

I have to admit that showed presence of mind. Mac put the car in gear, and we screamed off along the Budapester Strasse with Harold bleeding heavily. I grabbed his fine handkerchief out of his breast pocket and pressed it against his shoulder, only to have the cloth turn red almost instantly. "He needs a doctor!" I shouted.

Now that he knew I spoke English, Mac showed his true abilities. "Take his shirt off," he said, and when I had accomplished that—not very easily, given that I probably had broken ribs and Harold was half-conscious—he told me to use the shirt to put pressure on the wound. I managed this, but within minutes the white linen began to turn an ominous pink and then red.

"He's still bleeding," I said, my voice rising in alarm.

Mac's response was to step on the gas, endangering trams and carts and other cars to get us to the embassy, an overblown mansion with big pillars and a passage that took the car straight into a basement garage. Mac jumped out and ran to a house phone, summoning help that arrived in the form of two stout military types and what appeared to be a bona fide doctor. They wrestled Harold out of the car, put him on a stretcher, and rushed him along the corridor to an elevator.

I was left standing barefoot and bareheaded in a ruined frock beside the car, and it's likely I'd have been put out on the street if Mac had not taken charge of me. My own shoes and my leather coat were long gone. All I had were Muriel's ruined duds, totally unsuitable for my new identity card, and the few marks that remained from my trip to Grünberg's. Now that we were safe, I was freezing cold and shaking with nerves.

"Come on, lad." Mac spoke in a friendly sort of way, but when he patted my back, he sent pain all across my left side. "Ribs," was his diagnosis. "I can strap them up for you."

I followed him down the long corridor to a small, cozy room with a tartan rug and a narrow bed covered with a khaki blanket. He helped me take off Muriel's ruined clothes and produced some tape to protect my ribs. With this operation complete, he opened a bottle of whiskey and poured each of us a stiff tot. "None of that schnapps rubbish," he said.

I sat down on his bed, quite exhausted, while he opened the closet and rummaged in his trunk for a pair of khaki pants that were only two or three sizes too large and an olive-colored sweater with leather patches at the shoulders that made me look like a juvenile commando.

"Not quite right with the lipstick," I said.

He laughed. "You'd be surprised. Soldiers come in all varieties. Especially irregulars." He ran some water in his sink and brought me a cloth to wash my face. "Rest here while I organize a room for you. Better if you are not seen."

I lay down on his bed and slept until he returned. Outside it was totally dark. The streetlights were on, and the sounds of the city traffic diminished. He set a plate of stew and a cup of coffee on the bedside table. When I asked him what time it was, he said just half past nine. "Shock," he added. "It makes you tired."

"You know a lot about injuries."

"I was a medical orderly. Believe me, you can pick up quite a bit around field hospitals." He poured himself another whiskey and added a jigger in my coffee. "Medicinal," he said and winked.

Mac's kind good nature was so surprising that I wondered if there was some hidden agenda. Perhaps he detected my suspicion, because he said, "You saved the major's life."

"Just quicker reflexes is all."

"No, he'd have been a goner. His right eye was injured at Ypres. He claims to see motion, but between you and me, he's got no depth perception, and he'd have been blindsided today. Not that you'd ever mention that."

"Certainly not," I said. Nan had, after all, raised me to be a gentleman.

To seal the deal, Mac poured me another glass of whiskey, and we might have spent a congenial evening if there hadn't been a knock on the door. A smart young officer looked in and said, "The major's asking for you and for our guest."

Mac nodded. "A good sign," he said. We were escorted to the elevator and up to a top-floor bedroom. The officer tapped on the door, opened it, and stepped aside for us. The opening revealed a lot of High Victorian mahogany, brocade drapes, and stucco work centered on a large and ornate bed. Harold was propped up on pillows with thick bandages covering his right shoulder and upper arm. He had a tube in his left arm hooked up to a bottle hanging off a medical rack, and he looked pale and uncomfortable.

"How are you feeling, sir?" Mac asked.

"Surviving." Harold gestured for him to take the chair next to the bed. "We have a problem," he said. His eyes were half-closed.

"The film is good and being developed," Mac said. "You needn't worry about that."

Harold patted the bed, and Mac leaned in. "Who knew I was meeting Francis?"

"You and I. The switchboard might have guessed." He pursed his lips and added, "Plus whoever saw the car going out. There are always people around."

"And you," Harold said, looking at me. "Who knew?"

"My friend who phoned for me. But she is English."

Harold made a face that suggested no one was above suspicion. "Did anyone follow you?"

"Not that I know of. I've been cautious. Some of Uncle Lastings's enemies have been interested."

"Tell us where you spent last night," Mac said.

"With my friend. Who doesn't want to be involved."

Mac was going to press the issue, but Harold waved his hand. "We can worry about her later. My sense is that it's someone here. Support staff most likely, but you never know."

Mac was all efficiency and authority, which I thought odd for a chauffeur. "We'll put a guard on your room, sir. Close off this floor to all German nationals."

Harold considered this and shook his head. "Would cause talk. We will just be careful, though a guard is a good idea. But was I the real target? Or was it young Francis here? Without that ludicrous costume, would he have even made it to the café? We need to know that, too."

I caught the urgency in his voice. "I could leave Germany immediately," I offered, and my heart lifted as I envisioned my first flight. I would enjoy the drama of an early morning departure and the view of Germany from the clouds. What would that look like?

"Not possible," Harold said curtly. "Then there's the matter of your uncle. I'm afraid we're going to require your help."

I sensed an appeal from king and country, neither of which had shown much interest in me before. "What is my uncle up to?"

"Ah," said Harold. "That's something we'd all like to know."

CHAPTER EIGHT

I'd hoped to learn more about Uncle Lastings, but the only information I got was that Harold really was a major and that his name was actually Sutton. I know this because just as he was about to brief me, a doctor arrived with boards on his shoulders and bars on his sleeves and a great air of medical authority to declare that it was time for Major Sutton's shot. When Harold protested, the doctor, said, "No nonsense, Felix."

On the way downstairs, Mac explained that *Harold* was what he called the major's "operations name," and he'd assumed it just for me. I tried not to let that go to my head.

Down on the lower floor, Mac made a noisy deal of moving me into an isolated room close to the garage, followed by our very quiet return to his own room, where I was to spend the night. "No point in being careless," Mac said. "No one will touch you here."

I guessed that was right, but after my formidable keeper left, I wedged a chair under the doorknob just in case.

In the morning, I was as stiff as my own grandpa and black,

blue, and greenish-yellow all along one side. It took me a while to get dressed and longer than I liked to find my way down to the WC. When I got back, Mac was waiting for me with the information that Grünberg, the elderly pawnbroker, had been robbed yesterday. "The old man might have been killed," Mac said, "if it wasn't for a customer who arrived with several hunting rifles to pawn."

I tried to conceal my alarm at this news. "Pawnshops and banks. They're where the money is."

"The thieves were apparently looking for a camera. I think it must have been the one we redeemed."

"Luckily you have the film, so the camera is no use to anyone. And neither am I."

"Don't be too sure about that," Mac said. Promising me breakfast, he told me to stay in his room and out of sight.

My own thought was to see if any of his shoes fit me and whether he'd left any money lying around. I had in mind to make a quick departure, and I was headed for the door, when I realized that I did not have my new identity card. Where was it? In the pocket of Muriel's maroon frock. And where was that? Whisked away by Mac, who had a military affection for the clean and tidy. Just the same, I had almost made up my mind to run when he returned carrying a tray with tea, toast, a boiled egg, and a little dish of marmalade.

He glanced at the shoes. "You wouldn't get far, you know."

I shrugged. He was kind enough, but I didn't feel guilty.

"Eat up and then we'll talk to the major. Oh, and clothes are coming. We'll see about shoes later."

I suspected that all this was being laid on for some reason, but I didn't discover what for until we got upstairs. Harold was looking slightly better. The tube-and-bottle affair was gone and only scraps were left on his breakfast tray. Mac put it out in the hall and set two chairs close to the bed.

"How are you feeling?" Harold asked me.

"Battered," I said.

"You should feel fortunate. The film is useful. They would have killed you for it."

"They are ex-Freikorps, I think." I told them about the men who had come to Fritz's flat, but I omitted the address and Fritz's name and the Schmitt family business. They didn't need to know about that—or that I had a safe haven there if I needed one.

"A bayonet!" Mac said. "Well done."

Harold narrowed his eyes like a cat and said that it would have been best if I had come straight to the embassy. Or at least avoided the Adlon. "We had an agent in place," he said. "We would have recovered the camera before morning."

"And I would have been flat broke in Berlin."

"Your uncle is somewhat feckless," Harold admitted.

"He is a con man. Whyever do you employ him?"

Harold made a face, a subtle contraction of his mouth and chin. "You can't be too fussy in the defense of the realm. Your uncle has contacts we need, and he is trusted by people we could not otherwise approach. Besides, we go back a long way. Friend-ships in wartime . . ." He paused for a moment. I've learned that people who've been close to some profound, true thing are reluctant—or unable—to explain it. Maybe that's why there are painters. "Well"—Harold flapped his hand the way he did to dismiss objections or the objectionable—"you learn whom you can trust with the big things. Small things one learns to disregard."

Like fraud and entangling your nephew in a murder inquiry, I thought. So much in Berlin was a matter of perspective. "Now that you have your film, can I return to London?"

"We have some film," Harold said.

Uh-oh, I thought.

"We do not have all the information we would like."

I could hear Nan in my ear saying, *You'll want a lot less with more ease*, but I was clearly learning discretion because I kept my mouth shut.

Harold put on his most serious face, an expression that I saw Mac mirror—moment of truth! "Your uncle has disappeared. We've entirely lost contact with him."

"That's hardly unusual for Uncle Lastings. He hasn't been sending me postcards, either."

Harold leaned back on his pillows and shifted his wounded arm awkwardly. Mac rose to help, but Harold flapped his hand, determined to finish our conference. He had gone very white again. He gave whatever he wanted to say a moment's thought and exchanged a significant glance with Mac before he said, "You are aware of the terms of the Versailles agreement?"

Oh, right. In my recent circles we talked about little else, though I realized that Fritz's father had gone on about the betrayal of the army and sang "Watch on the Rhine" when he was drunk. "Indemnities, the Rhineland?" I guessed.

"Correct. And German demilitarization. Very important for

our French allies, along with the Saar coal and Alsace-Lorraine. His Majesty's Government is also vitally interested in all attempts of the Weimar Republic to rearm."

"But hasn't their military been limited? How many men can they legitimately have?"

"A hundred thousand. Seven infantry divisions, three cavalry."

That sounded to me like a great many soldiers.

"They were also supposed to get rid of the general military staff. We suspect that they have simply reorganized. Similarly, although they did disband the Freikorps, paramilitary groups are building under the cover of veterans organizations, sports, and youth groups like the Wandervogel. They're analogous to our scouts."

The penny dropped. "Uncle Lastings claimed to be funneling money to some of those outfits. Thanks to funds from the Society for a Christian Europe."

"A society that exists mostly in the mind of your uncle. But fear of the Reds is very real. The Weimar government sees Bolsheviks under the bed and so favors the right-wing fighters over the workers parties. Your uncle," he added dryly, "perceived an opening into the shadow armies that could be profitable to all sides. You must admit that took some doing."

"So he was gathering information for you. Taking photographs of what?"

"Installations, gatherings, documents."

"And they were onto him? So he shot two of them?"

Harold nodded. "We don't know exactly, but that is a likely scenario."

I honestly wondered when he'd had the time. With a lot of ex-Freikorps men on his tail, my uncle would not have much freedom to photograph secret documents. "He will be on the run. How is that useful to you?"

"He has other material. We know that. He only needs a safe way to deliver it. Once we know where he is, of course."

I'd thought that my life—and my uncle's—was rackety and improvisational, but it was nothing like His Majesty's secret service or whatever they were called.

"We need someone in plain sight," Harold said. "Someone he'll spot and who'll set up a contact for us. That's all that's needed."

"And where would this be? He told me that he was leaving Berlin. He could be anywhere. He could be cooling his heels in London, for all I know."

"He is still in Germany. We know that he has not reentered the United Kingdom." Harold seemed very sure about this, but then he should know with his knowledge of passports and border crossings. "We suspect he is still in the Berlin area. He has friends."

"You'd be better to enlist one of them," I said. "My German is still weak. It's obvious I'm foreign, and that police sketch has been in the papers. Besides, I don't know anything about armies or politics."

"Your father was a soldier," Harold said. "He fought in the Boer War."

"The Boer War was a long time ago, and nothing about my father inclines me toward the military."

Harold raised his eyebrows, and there was a brief but heavy silence.

"If you won't send me home, give me that identity card. I'll make my own way."

"Sit down," Harold said. "You are known to dangerous people, and I assume you won't always have a bayonet handy. Mac and I have devised a plan. You should listen to it."

"I should leave." I stood up and held out my hand. "You promised me papers. You've gotten the film."

"Right you are," said Mac. He took the identity card out of his pocket and handed it over. "I give you a day. Two at the most."

"What do you mean?"

"The Kripos, of course."

"We like to be cooperative," Harold said in a weary tone as if this was all something I should understand already. "The police would be interested in your whereabouts. And if we couldn't tell them that, we could at least enlighten them about your new identity."

"Nods as good as a wink to them," Mac added. "All that about Prussian discipline and efficiency? Perfectly true. I didn't believe it myself at first."

Harold cleared his throat. "In fairness to you, we should simply keep you here. Of course, you're free to go, and you have papers, but if we should lose sight of you, I have Bernard Weiss's personal phone number." He gave a faint smile. "An interesting character—a Jew, a Prussian, and a cop all in one."

I sat back down, wondering if Nan would classify this as a blackmail, extortion, or a protection racket.

"There's a good lad," said Mac. "We don't want to see you hurt."

"I wouldn't need to be hurt! There are daily flights from Tempelhof to London."

"We have a budget, you know," Harold said. "The Leica rather depleted the incidentals kitty for the moment."

I'll bet, I thought, but I didn't say anything. As Nan used to tell me, *If you can't say anything nice, keep your mouth shut.* Who would have thought that my peculiar education would prove so useful?

"You perhaps have wondered," Harold began after a moment, "why your uncle was so fond of visiting the Eldorado? Given that he had no interest in wearing women's clothes or in men who did."

"My uncle would roger anyone," I said.

"We are aware of his somewhat catholic tastes, but trust me, even Lastings had his limits."

"All right," I said. "Lingerie and feathers were not in his wardrobe. So what?"

"Yet he always made time for a quick visit to the Eldorado, didn't he?"

"He liked lively nightspots. He enjoyed the cabaret there."

"That's right. And some of his contacts also liked the Eldorado. What better way to hide in plain sight?"

Talk about the rabbit hole. I'd realized that my uncle was a con man and a tomcat. Now it appeared that he ran some sort of spy ring peopled by chaps who liked to put on rouge and heels and dance with the "hostesses" at the Eldorado. Or perhaps they were

the hostesses at the Eldorado. I seemed to remember Uncle Lastings taking the floor occasionally, *just to be polite.*

"Your stratagem the other day suggested a safe place for you."

I thought that my next letter to Nan would certainly be full
of interest. Defending my life with bayonets and high heels, con-
sorting with both thugs and spies. She hadn't been kidding when
she said that travel was an education, but I was beginning to
think I should have stuck to my books. I could be translating
Greek plays and passing notes to pretty third formers and doing
nothing more strenuous than fielding out by the cricket bound-
ary. "What's in it for you?" I asked.

"Information, of course. With you in place at the cabaret, we
hope some of your uncle's contacts will emerge."

"It seems a pretty forlorn hope!"

"Your uncle is in serious danger. He has twice put himself at
the service of his country, and we are sure the information he is
obtaining is of great importance. We are asking you to work for
a time at the Eldorado. Hardly trench warfare."

Ah, the superiority of the ex-military. "I'm hardly a soldier,
and I suspect my country would just as soon lock me up."

"All the more reason," Mac broke in, "to build up a little useful credit."

There was that. And I did owe Uncle Lastings some interesting experiences. "I hate music, and I can't dance. Especially not
in women's heels."

"We're not expecting you to rival Hansi Sturm," Harold said,
mentioning the reining diva of the drag clubs. "No, no, no. And
the proprietor of the Eldorado is most fussy about his hostesses.

Trains them like geishas, I'm told. It was a great concession on his part even to consider you for the hatcheck counter."

Checking hats and coats. All right. It sounded useless to me, but it could be worse. I could be stuck in the embassy or, worse, in some Prussian correctional institution. "If I do this, how will Uncle Lastings's contacts recognize me? How will they possibly know?"

"They won't," Harold said. "You'll have to spot them."

CHAPTER NINE

Dear Nan,

I am gainfully employed, checking hats and coats in an interesting club.

Interesting certainly covered the Eldorado, which featured satin and feathers like a posh wedding and, on certain afternoons, enough tweeds and brogues with the lesbian crowd to clothe a grouse shoot.

There's a dress code, and I hardly think you'd recognize me when I'm behind my counter. But I have been kitted out gratis, so I've saved a little money.

All true. Mac had disappeared for a couple of hours and returned with two complete sets of clothing. Pants, a shirt, a leather jacket, and a pair of sturdy shoes, plus a cocktail dress, heels, a hat, a short coat and, yes, a very nice pair of silk stockings. The dress fit, and if I still found heels tricky, these were a good deal more comfortable than Muriel's. Mac also brought a cosmetic kit, a new razor and shaving cream, and a brush, along with a neat little suitcase, neither too smart nor too shabby, to hold the lot.

When I was dressed with my face made up, we went aloft for Harold's inspection. He was wearing his smart diplomat's trousers and shoes but still had a pajama shirt over his bandages. "Let me see you walk," he said.

I obliged. The whole thing was so like a ridiculous costume party that I couldn't help getting into the spirit of it.

"What do you think?" Mac asked.

"I think that a good sergeant can work wonders." He nodded to me and added, "The army runs on its non-coms."

He might have given me a little credit, especially since I did my own eyes, but this was not the time to complain, because Mac had slipped me a few marks and promised to pay for my room.

I have quite a nice room—and get this, Nan: My landlady is English! What do you think about that?

Actually, I knew quite well what she would think: that her dear boy had rejoined respectability and civilization. Which was partly true. The landlady was Miss Clarice Fallowfield, unless, like Harold, she had a selection of monikers, and she might have, since I suspect she was employed by the embassy.

Miss Fallowfield is tall, pale, and angular, with large hands.

She has a long nose on a thin, aristocratic face and she has
splendid manners.

That was on the one side—the pearls and cardigan side. On
the other, she smoked like a chimney and, when the occasion
required, could swear like a sailor. She and Mac were old and
trusted friends; I guessed from the war, for wherever else would
debutante material like my landlady have met a slater from
Glasgow? I'd noticed a picture on her living-room mantel showing four women beside a military ambulance. I thought she was
one of them, back when her hair was still dark.

Anyway, she and Mac understood each other, for they said
very little when they met—a glance, a nod, *a very good* was all
they needed to settle whatever needed to be decided. That was
mostly, at the moment, about me. House rules: I was to come
directly back after my shift at the Eldorado. There would be, in
Miss Fallowfield's words, *a great hue and cry* if I was not in on the
dot. This was *for my own protection.*

Of course, I would be a lot better protected back in Soho, but
Miss Fallowfield took a strong line on duty, as in *England expects*
every man to do, etc. Fortunately, she also ran a comfortable establishment with very decent food. She was amused by my working clothes and supplemented the initial frock with a couple of
dresses cut down from her own wardrobe. Very Edwardian, very
long, very old-fashioned.

When I pointed this out, she said, "It's all costume, Francis.
See if the punters don't like a little variety."

I was embarrassed to say that she was right. The plum velvet proved a particular favorite, and I came back the first night I wore it with my little evening reticule—another present from Miss Fallowfield—loaded with tips. She was also sympathetic to my struggles with high heels. *You need boots, Francis. They provide better ankle support.* Too bad the Eldorado was strictly elegant footwear and that boots—particularly high ones with lots of buttons—were associated with a particularly notorious set of prostitutes.

Other house rules: no boyfriends—no girlfriends, either, although I thought Miss Fallowfield might like the raffish Muriel. Afternoons I sallied out to one of the boy bars, and sometimes I was lucky and sometimes I was bored. But either way, by six o'clock, I was back at the flat turning myself into Dolly, the new and delightful English hatcheck girl, and by seven, I was at the Eldorado. I stayed on until three in the morning, when I usually shared a taxi home with Sabine, one of the hostesses.

Sabine was slight with narrow shoulders and long legs. The first thing she did in the taxi was take off her shoes and give a sigh like a weary horse. Suddenly, Sabine was halfway back to Sigi. "How many miles do you think, Francis?" He'd ask me every night, for though he told me (and I believed it was true) that he lived for the evenings at the Eldorado, he found the endless rounds of the dance floor with the heavy-footed clientele wearying.

At first I thought he fancied me, and then I hoped he might be Uncle Lastings's elusive contact, but no. He just liked to chat. As Sabine, he'd talk to me about clothes and makeup. He was catty about my hand-me-downs from Miss Fallowfield; at the same time, he couldn't keep his hands off the velvet frock—or the nice party silk, either.

"Prewar! What I wouldn't give for a few yards of that. Do tell me where you got it! I know you have a secret source," and so on. Back to Sigi, he complained about his feet and discussed the fortunes of Hertha Berlin, the football club, and his prospects of seeing the Nürburgring, the new auto racetrack. I found him as interesting as just about anyone I wouldn't want to go to bed with, and I could assure Miss Fallowfield that my feminine version had a safe escort home.

She did ask occasionally, and I got the sense that she was not just a nosey landlady but actually felt responsible for me in some way. Did that give me a good feeling? It did not. Suggesting, as it did, that I was still in a pickle and would be until Uncle Lastings's spy circle—or whatever they were—broke cover and told me all about remilitarization and dodgy fighters.

I wrote only some of this to Nan, whom I didn't want to worry. I did tell her that I was certainly seeing the nightlife of Berlin. Yes, indeed. Hats and coats and furs and scarves in and out. Portly types—ex-profiteers to a man—clucked me under the chin and asked what a sweet young thing like me was doing at the Eldorado. Visitors asked if I missed England and tried to pinch my bum. Folk of all persuasions drank too much and leaned on my counter and told me their troubles, no doubt because the barmen had gotten sick of them.

The customers shouted for their clothes and lost their tickets. Coming and going they were always in a hurry, and some of them were too mean to tip the attendant. I'd even had one or two accuse me of damaging their coats or mislaying their hats. The tourists were the worst. They'd been taken to the Eldorado with a promise of depravity, so they felt they could forget their manners and hold on to their wallets. You get the picture.

Still, much interest. For one thing, I kept waiting for Uncle Lastings's contact—if there was such a person. One of the barmen? One of the waiters? The manager, Herr K., who had so kindly taken me on? Or one of the hostesses, all of whom seemed as preoccupied with their feuds and quarrels and struggles for precedence as a bunch of dowagers. Who in this lot could I trust? Dare I drop a hint? I had many more questions than answers.

But, there was some compensation for the low-level suspense and the long hours in torturous heels. A nice client would bring over a drink or compliment me on my makeup or on my frock. It turned out that Sabine wasn't the only one with an eye for pre-war fabric. And then some of the real queens were living works of art, substitutes for the paintings in the galleries that I used to enjoy and that I now had to avoid.

Being at the Eldorado, I got so used to the drag artistes that it was sometimes a surprise to be talking to Miss Fallowfield or see women on the street and suddenly find them rather small and tame-looking. That was the Eldorado effect, where, as Belinda told me one day, *life is larger than life.*

Certainly that was true in her case. In full kit with heels, she was maybe six three or six four. Add the diamond tiara (fake but well done) with the ostrich plume and she was closing in on seven feet. Unlike Sigi, I was not sure Belinda ever lived in the masculine mode. Even in the cramped lavatory, where she touched up her makeup, or back in my booth, where she sometimes took her cigarette breaks, she was always the same: large and flamboyant and feminine.

She sang quite well, and she danced even better. Her tango was a thing of beauty, and when all six feet plus of her got going on the Charleston, believe me, she deserved the applause. She was learning English—the better to entrance the tourists—and she liked to practice on me. *Vell, dolling, how are you today?* she'd say, and I would help her with the elusive English *W* and repeat polite turns of phrase for her, because she really was courteous.

Belinda hated swearing and vulgar talk. She was not just a lady but a lady from before the war, and her great passion was hats. Knowing I was English, one day she asked me if I had ever been to Ascot *vith ze vonderful hats.*

Then I made a mistake. "Not Ascot, but other race meetings," I said, momentarily forgetting that I was Francis Wood and not the son of a race trainer who had grown up within a stone's throw of the Curragh.

Belinda gave me a sly side-glance. "Really," she said. "And hats. They have ze big hats there, too?"

"Sometimes," I said. "Sometimes in Ireland."

She winked. "Ve must talk," she said. "About ze hats of Ireland." Then she swanned back out to the dance floor and returned to work, leaving me nervous. Which was silly, really. I hadn't asked to be a junior spy, and the powers that be had to expect some mistakes. Just the same, I wasn't quite as confident as I'd been, and my uneasiness only increased when Sabine insisted on paying for the cab that night and spent most of the ride complaining about Belinda, that treacherous bitch, who seemed to have given Sabine reason to feel deep offense over the favors of a rich Argentinean. You can bet I offered no opinion one way or the other.

Then, the next night, quite late, Belinda stopped by my counter and handed me a pack of cigarettes. "A little thank-you, dolling, for my English lessons."

"Thanks, but I don't—" I started to say I didn't smoke, that cigarettes were death on my asthma, before I caught myself. Here it was, and from the most unexpected courier! My long-awaited message from Uncle Lastings and my exit from Berlin. "Don't need anything," I finished. "It's always a pleasure to talk with you. But thanks." And with a hasty glance into the hall and toward the dance floor, I stuck the cigarettes into the front of my dress and fluffed up the lace collar to hide the bulge.

"It's always a pleasure to talk with you," Belinda repeated carefully. "I can say that to any gentleman?"

"Oh, yes. It's very polite." I'd been tempted once or twice to teach her something that would make a gentleman really take notice, but now I was glad I'd resisted. Under her feathers and tiara and pounds of kohl and rouge, Belinda turned out to be braver and more interesting than I'd imagined.

So, success! *My work, Nan, has turned out to be more interesting than I expected, and I am doing well.* For the rest of my shift, the cigarette pack lay against my collarbone like a hot potato, and I couldn't keep from fussing with the neck of the dress and tugging at the bodice to keep everything smooth. I had my coat on before the hour struck and legged it out of the club and into a cab before Sabine could follow. Not smart, I realized once I was in the taxi, but Sabine was always alert and nosey, and I was sure she would have sensed that I had something to hide. I decided that the next evening, I would have to use an excuse—sudden illness.

Back at Miss Fallowfield's apartment, I tapped lightly on her door, unsure whether I was to wake her. She replied instantly, and I found her sitting up on her bed reading but fully dressed.

"What is it, Francis?"

"I think it's what you've been waiting for." I handed her the cigarette pack. "A present from—"

"No names at this point," said Miss Fallowfield quickly. "Best for you to know and not me. Sound procedure. Everyone knows only two links in the chain. That's what's called a *cutout*."

"Right." My education was proceeding apace. "The cigarettes are supposedly for helping with her English, though she knows I cannot smoke."

Miss Fallowfield raised her eyebrows and turned the packet over carefully. "Thank you, Francis. I will have a little look at this, and we will talk in the morning."

That, if nothing else, dispelled the notion that Miss Clarice Fallowfield was just another impoverished gentlewoman renting spare rooms. The next morning, I was not entirely surprised to find Mac at the breakfast table, tucking into sausage and eggs under the blue haze of Miss Fallowfield's cigarettes.

"Ah, the man of the hour."

I suspected that she was being sarcastic, but then I was

congratulated so heartily that I thought I might be able to start packing my case. "The material is valuable then? And authentic?"

"Oh, it's from Lastings all right," Miss Fallowfield said. "No question about that. He wants money. Claims *dire need*, as per usual."

That did sound like Uncle Lastings.

"Useful information, though," Mac said.

"Yes, what we have. Funds are needed to secure what he calls *more and better intelligence*."

That was the Lastings's touch all right, but his language was quite subdued compared to his communications with the Society for a Christian Europe in which his activities were always described in the most colorful terms. Here, he was dealing with pros.

"And are you going to pay for more?"

Mac shrugged and looked at Miss Fallowfield. "Will Harold agree?" she asked.

"I think so," Mac said.

"The money will have to go back via Francis's contact."

"But surely I'm leaving! Mac can go. Anyone can go. Wasn't that the whole point of choosing the Eldorado—that strangers are a commonplace?"

"Simplicity," said Miss Fallowfield, "is a cardinal virtue."

Mac took out a fat envelope. "For your contact."

"I can't just hand that over. You don't know how jealous and nosey and competitive the whole club is. Why, half of Berlin would know within the hour."

"But you're a clever boy," Mac said. "You'll think of something."

I argued about this and said a lot of stupid things that changed nothing. Mac and Harold had my passport. The police had my name and my picture. Father Brotz's dangerous friends had me in their sights. I sulked and ate more than my share of the sausages, while Mac drank cups of tea and Miss Fallowfield smoked as if her life depended on it. Finally I said, "Can you buy me a book of English grammar? Or an English-language phrasebook?"

"That would do. There is a good bookstore on the Ku'damn," Miss Fallowfield said. "But best let Mac buy it. And I will fix it nicely for you. You'll be perfectly safe giving a language book as a little present to your contact."

CHAPTER TEN

I set off for the Eldorado in a bad mood, even though Mac had slipped me twenty marks, enough for an hour in the Tiergarten with a boy I knew and a decent early supper. But things couldn't have gone more smoothly. Miss Fallowfield had secreted the money cleverly toward the back of *The New English Primer*. "The grammar part will still be usable that way," she remarked. And instead of wrapping paper, she added a ribbon and a bow. "So it's obvious what it is," she said, "but still a present."

Right. Belinda squealed with delight and tried out all her new phrases until we wound up laughing in the coat-check booth and were rebuked by Herr K., the manager. With that, I perked up, and once again saw the amusing side of this long-running costume party. So I really wasn't prepared when, two nights later, Herr K. stormed up to the coat-check booth around eight and demanded to know where my friend Belinda was hiding.

"She hasn't come in yet, *mein Herr*."

"I don't like it!" he said. "I don't like it at all. If she's late again, she gets the sack." He stomped around and swore so that Sabine started snickering and several of the other hostesses waved their fans and fluffed their feathers and pretended to be shocked.

"Perhaps she's taken ill," I said. "She was complaining of a headache last night."

"She's never ill!" Herr K. almost screamed. "She's gone off with some fool who'll break her heart and then what use will she be? My best hostess ever, and she has the brain of a flea."

Naturally, he was exaggerating, but he was so upset that I kept an eye out for her. When nine o'clock came, she still had not arrived, although the club was filling up and the dance floor was crowded. It was not like Belinda to miss out on good tips, and I began to worry.

Around ten, during a lull, I asked Martha, the pale and probably tubercular cigarette girl, if she would watch the coat-check booth for a few minutes so that I could get some air. Some nights I needed to clear my lungs after the oppressive smoke in the room. In return, Martha would give me a few coins to purchase what she called her "little pick-me-up" from the neighborhood cocaine dealer.

I found him farther down the street than usual, young and handsome and blond with a posh manner that suggested a precipitous descent from respectable wealth to street-level drug dealing. This sort of transformation was by no means unusual in Berlin, where decently dressed old women scoured the gutters after the vegetable carts, and every other corner had its mutilated war vet.

After we chatted for a few minutes, I pocketed Martha's deck of snow and strolled back toward the club. I was a block away when I stopped to take a leak in an alley, figuring anywhere would be cleaner than the miserable WC Herr K. kept for the staff. But as I stepped into the shadows, something caught my eye. Bright, winking in the streetlight, and ending with a plume. I had the nasty feeling that it was Belinda's tiara. I bent down. Yes, the ornament certainly looked like it. "Belinda?"

No answer. I moved farther down the alley into real darkness and nearly stumbled over something large but not entirely hard. I couldn't make myself put my hand down, and I stepped back. As my shadow moved, some light from the streetlamp ran like a shiver down a satin skirt, touched a silk stocking, and died on the tip of a patent leather shoe.

"Belinda? Belinda!"

I edged around, keeping the light on the body, because there was no doubt now: Someone was lying there, and I feared it was her. Alive or dead? *Alive, please!* I bent to touch her shoulder. Large and solid. Surely too large and solid to be dead. "Belinda!"

Go ahead, Francis. I touched her face and found it cold. Was it really cold or just my hands? *Feel her neck.* The big pulse in the neck—that's the test. *So feel her neck,* which meant touching her skin again, the skin that was cold—at least cool. I took a deep breath and wheezed. *Just nerves,* I told myself, because I had to reach down and touch her neck to find the pulse, the pulse that would be there, signaling she was all right, fine, *tickety-boo,* as Uncle Lastings would say. What on earth had made him select Belinda, who loved hats, who approached seven feet tall in full regalia? I thrust my hand down, searching for the artery, her pulse, her life—nothing.

Heartbeat. She had to have a heartbeat. I put my hand down on her satin bodice and swore. My hand was wet. When I held it up to the light, I saw a deeper darkness that threatened my ridiculous clothing. "Help!" The word was a croak. "*Helfen Sie mir!*" Right language but still no air, no breath, no voice.

I staggered to the street. There would have to be police. I must alert Herr K., who would summon the Kripos. Who would arrive with questions for me. A disaster, because I did not think that my papers would hold up for a murder investigation, especially not when another English visitor of my general height, age, and coloring was already wanted as an accessory in a capital case.

No indeed. If they questioned me, the jig would be up. I didn't need Nan to tell me that! *Ergo*—as my old Latin teacher used to say—*ergo*, no police. But to abandon Belinda in the alley was frightful. She had been a friend, a harmless friend, who loved fancy hats and polite gentlemen and lived with who knows what hopes and fantasies. I felt so sick that I threw up in the gutter and had to find a puddle to wash my hands. Under the nearest streetlight, I checked my frock for blood and mess, then caught my breath. I must return to the club, where Dolly of the hat-check counter must be her usual vivacious self with her amusing German. Could I manage that? First, I thought yes, and then I thought no. Then I thought of efficient Prussian police and grim Prussian jails and not-to-be-imagined Prussian reformatories, and I got almost to the door when I remembered that Belinda might have been carrying some papers for Uncle Lastings.

What if she was? What if they were found? Would there be incriminating names? I hustled back down the street, my shoes—instruments of the devil—clattering on every step and cutting into the backs of my heels. At the alley, I stopped and looked both ways. Was that the dealer with his little decks of snow? Far down the street? Was he liable to talk to the police? I didn't think so.

Just the same, it took a few moments more before I could enter the alley, find Belinda's corpse, and touch her skirt. Nothing in the pocket. Her coat next. One pocket was available. Nothing. The other was under her body. *Pull it out, pull it up. Anything?* No. I didn't need to worry. She'd had nothing. She'd delivered the cash, and Uncle Lastings had taken it and turned it into dinners for some rich widow. I could go back.

I stood up, wheezing and shaking. I remembered Belinda sashaying up to the coat-check counter and handing me the cigarette pack. She hadn't been wearing a coat. So nothing in her coat pocket. And she hadn't taken it from her skirt, either. Like a Victorian lady, she'd reached into her décolletage and pulled out the package.

I felt sick again and put my hand over my mouth. But if she was carrying anything, it would be in the bodice of her dress. Which was soaked in blood. In the end, I took out my handkerchief, wrapped it around my index finger, and carefully poked at her bodice. Was that a crackle, a faint papery rustle? Papers or just the "gay deceivers" that were part of Belinda's astonishing transformation? With great care, I lifted the edge of the dress by one armhole and fished out, yes, a pack of cigarettes.

I stuck it into my dress, and after a cautious exit from the alley, I went straight to the Eldorado before I could lose heart. Inside, Martha was pouting—"her pick-me-up" had been delayed. Herr K. was still swearing about Belinda's absence, and it was all I could do to keep from striking him out of grief and shame at my own cowardice. Sabine was swanning around, Queen of the

Dance Floor for once, and I had a very strong urge to puke up everything I had ever eaten.

But the café was busy. Coats were wanted immediately, others were flung on the counter to be checked. Hats came in with scarves and fancy fur wraps. I tried to think of nothing but tickets and numbers and to see nothing but collars and sleeves and bowler hats. I said nothing but *Ja, mein Herr* and *Dankeschön, Fräulein* and counted the minutes until I could put on my coat. I was so anxious to leave that I forgot the little evening reticule that held my tips. I went back behind the counter for it, a delay that landed me in a cab with Sabine, the very last person, saving a cop, that I cared to see.

Naturally she was full of what she called "the scandal of the evening," Belinda's absence. Not unprecedented, Sabine assured me. "She's run off with a fellow, you'll see." I shrugged and said nothing, but I wondered if that could be a positive. Could it have been what the Germans so expressively call a *Lustmürder*? A crime of passion with nothing to do with Uncle Lastings or me? A nice idea, but I couldn't quite convince myself, not even with Sabine, shoes off now and wig askew, telling me about previous Belinda escapades. "She's looking for true love," Sabine said contemptuously.

"Aren't we all?"

"Darling, not at the Eldorado!" She burst out laughing, and I had to fight an impulse to strangle her. Wanted for one killing and vulnerable to questioning about another—it would almost make sense to commit one for real, albeit in the back of a Berlin taxicab. You can see I was not in a normal frame of mind.

To save myself, I focused on everything else: the back of the seats, Sabine's pink-and-lavender makeup, and the lights shimmering on other cabs and winking in the puddles. I would remember it all down to the smallest detail, a trick I had learned years ago when I was the unhappy child of a disappointed family and there were lots of painful things to ignore. Sitting in the back of the cab, I worked to replace the dim shape, the faint glitter of the tiara, and the gossamer ostrich plume with the cracked leather of the cab seats, the wen on the back of the driver's neck, the angle of Sabine's knee in her green dress.

Look and don't listen, because Sabine's a malicious bitch. ". . . too close, I've thought, with Belinda . . . not the best reputation. And you know she's a Pole, probably a Jew. Why are people like that taking work from honest Germans, eh? That has to end. Sooner or later, we'll have it all back."

"What?" I asked finally. "What are you talking about?"

"Where have you been! The bastard Polish Republic and Silesia, of course. Hundreds of thousands of Germans in the east have been abandoned to Slavs and barbarism. We didn't fight four years to lose our ancestral lands to treachery and a treaty."

And so on. They'd been halfway to Moscow with the Brest-Litovsk Treaty, which apparently had been as much of a pact as Versailles was a scandal. The bastard republic had been mostly German; Danzig had been safe and *Mitteleuropa* free from Bolshevism. "All good things, right?"

"I'm not interested in politics," I said and signaled for the cabbie to stop. I never rode all the way to the flat, not with Sabine. With a quick *Gute Nacht*, I made a feint toward one of the tall houses clad in smoke-washed stones. Once the cab was out of sight, I walked back to the previous street and up to Miss Fallowfield's flat. I could not stomach talking about Belinda in fancy dress, so I changed my clothes before I knocked at my landlady's door.

She was as I had found her the other night: fully dressed but sitting up on her bed with a book. I laid the cigarette packet beside her. "It may be just cigarettes," I said.

She examined the stain on the packet along with my expression and immediately went to her kitchen, returning with two large tumblers of whiskey. "What happened?"

I told her about finding Belinda.

"What did you do, Francis?" Her voice was suddenly sharp, and I knew that she understood all the implications, including some beyond my imagination.

"Nothing. I washed off my hand and checked my dress for blood and went back inside."

"Good. That was the right thing to do. Difficult, but the right thing."

"It does not feel like the right thing at all. She cannot be left in the alley. The police must be notified."

"Indeed," said Miss Fallowfield, lighting a cigarette. "And so they shall be. But not by you. I will phone Mac, and he will arrange an anonymous tip."

The anonymous tip was a perennial in Nan's favorite crime stories, and I had to suppress a giggle. *Control the nerves, Francis!*

Miss Fallowfield took my empty glass through to the kitchen and returned with it full. And with a slice of dark bread and a piece of cheese.

"Tell me again, everything you remember," she said. "And anything else that might be useful."

By the time I finished, my head was aching.

"She was in her working clothes," Miss Fallowfield observed, "suggesting she was on her way to the club when she was attacked."

"Probably. I don't know. She seemed—she seemed to live the role. If you understand what I mean." It was all so sad and bizarre that I said, "Why on earth would Uncle Lastings have picked her? The most unlikely person!"

"Who is likely to be a patriot?" Miss Fallowfield asked. "Your friend's real name was Arek Jagoda, and he fought in the Battle of Warsaw."

"The Miracle on the Vistula?" That took some imagining. Take away the tiara, the oversize heels, the satin skirts, and silk stockings. Add a rifle with fixed bayonet or envision a cavalry-man's saber; I couldn't quite do it.

"That's right. He was with the Sixth Army, who turned the Reds back from Warsaw. We've been checking up on him. His military record appears quite genuine. As ex-Polish army, he would not have been eager to see the German military forces reconstituted."

"No, I can see that he wouldn't. I'm just having a hard time putting Belinda, whose great ambition was to visit Ascot in a garden-party hat, into anybody's front line."

"People are endlessly surprising," Miss Fallowfield said. "Especially in wartime. Especially *in extremis*." She stood up and went into the hallway, where I heard her calling Mac.

When she returned, she asked, "Could there be anyone in the club itself who would want to do her harm?"

"Just all the other hostesses. But not really. They're a catty, competitive bunch." And then I stopped, half-surprised.

"What is it?"

"Something Sabine said in the cab coming home. She was going on about politics. I was trying not to listen, but she shares the general hostility toward immigrants from the east. And she was talking about the treaties. And Poland. That's right. The territory of what she called the 'Bastard Republic' that should belong to Deutschland."

"Now that is interesting," Miss Fallowfield said.

I shrugged. "Half the Eldorado's clientele probably thinks the same."

"Were they otherwise on good terms, Belinda and this . . . Sabine?"

"Sabine, otherwise known as Sigi. Sigi Egger, I think it is. A different sort altogether. And no, they weren't on good terms. Belinda was . . ." I paused for a minute, too tired to put my thoughts in order. "There was something genuine about Belinda. She was ridiculously big and tall, and yet, she was glamorous and feminine and natural, if that is possible."

Miss Fallowfield shrugged. "Nature sometimes makes mistakes," she suggested.

"Maybe. And I think Belinda was goodhearted. Maybe that was it. She wasn't quite as hard and cynical as the usual item, so the others were jealous when people responded to that. Even the sort of people who go slumming at the Eldorado. Now she's lying dead in an alley," I said, and I suddenly hated Berlin, which had been such a respite, such fun, allowing me such freedom to be myself.

CHAPTER ELEVEN

By the time we were finished talking, I was semiconscious—a combination of shock, fatigue, and single-malt whiskey; Miss Fallowfield drank nothing but the best. She sent me to bed, and it was late the next morning before I became aware of voices in the flat—Mac's and Harold's to be exact. I pulled the covers over my head and tried to shut my ears. The murmur went on and on. Then the neighboring church clock struck an amazing number of times. Could it really be eleven?

There was nothing I could do. I had to get up. I put on my clothes and shuffled down to the WC, before, unshaven and hungover, I appeared in the kitchen.

Miss Fallowfield poured me a cup of coffee and presented a rack of toast. I looked at both and considered whether either would be a good idea.

"Eat," Mac said. "Good for shock. And for Miss F.'s whiskey."

"My medical advisor," I said sarcastically, but I sampled a slice of toast without ill effect.

"We're in a serious situation," Harold said.

That was pretty rich. He wasn't torturing his toes in Dolly's heels night after night. He had diplomatic immunity, so he didn't have to worry about the Kripos, and one of his coworkers wasn't lying dead in an alley.

"Normally, at this stage of an operation, we would remove all civilian personnel."

I figured I was "civilian personnel" and the word *normally* put the wind up. "Normally," I said. "What about abnormally?"

"The situation we find ourselves in at the moment does not allow for normal operating procedures."

"You're not sending me home," I guessed.

"Impossible at the moment. You cannot leave the Eldorado without becoming the prime suspect. Am I correct that you left the club for a time last night?"

"To get some air, yes. And," I added because it was sure to come to light, "to purchase a packet of cocaine for a coworker."

"So there is a witness to place you near the alley. That is most unfortunate, because dealers are vulnerable to coercion." Harold gave a sniff, as if this whole situation was my fault instead of his harebrained scheme.

"The body was cold. Belinda was expected at the club much earlier. She was supposed to be in no later than eight, ever. Herr K. was beside himself at her being so tardy. She'd certainly been dead quite a while before I found her."

"No one here suspects you, laddie," Mac said, "but we must understand the Kripos' thinking if we are to keep you safe."

"And useful," I said.

"It is rare," Miss Fallowfield said in her dry, clear voice, "that one is able to be useful to one's country."

"I'll be more useful alive, not lying in a pool of blood like Belinda."

"Belinda, or I should say Arek Jagoda, now rests in the Berlin morgue. He was found early this morning."

That was good to know, even if Harold's schoolmaster precision annoyed me. "About time," I said.

"The best we could do. Now," Harold said, fixing me with a glacial look, "it is vital that you return to the Eldorado tonight. That you be shocked and surprised at what will by then be the common knowledge of Belinda's death."

I didn't like that at all. Suddenly, the toast and coffee was a bad idea that set my stomach twitching. "If I am there, I will be questioned, because surely, they will talk to everyone. And as you say, I can be put near the alley."

"An alley you did not go into. You were wearing patent leather heels and a silk frock. Why you went in, I don't know."

"You haven't seen the Eldorado's staff WC," I said.

Mac cracked a smile at this. "Let's hope the police don't have to use it."

"My papers are phony, and the police have that damn drawing."

"Not a terribly good likeness," said Miss Fallowfield, dexterously lighting her new cigarette from the stub of her last.

"You must be interviewed in your working clothes." Mac's face told me that he wasn't joking. "No," he said to the others, "the boy's right. Even in an identity card photo, Francis Wood looks far too much like the missing Francis Bacon. And using the same given name was an error."

"We thought keeping your own first name would make it easier for you," Harold said. "We did not expect you to entangle yourself in a capital crime."

As if I'd gone out of my way! "All I want is to return to London. I didn't ask to go to work in the biggest transvestite night spot in the city."

"Where," Miss Fallowfield pointed out, "you have been successfully hiding in plain sight. It's a matter of nerve. Keep yours, stick with—Dolly, is it?—and you have a good chance of escaping police notice."

I must have looked as dubious as I felt, because she added, "Tears are often efficacious. Shed them liberally in tight spots."

I wondered if she had ever practiced that strategy. She seemed a singularly dry-eyed sort.

"But don't overdo it," Mac said. "A little work with the handkerchief goes a long way."

"I don't know that I'm much of an actor." I'd played the third shepherd in the Christmas pageant and one of the senatorial crowd in *Julius Caesar*. Neither seemed quite adequate preparation.

"You'll just have to do your best," said Harold, "because if you fail, you will wind up in custody, where I fear your documents cannot sustain you."

"Give me a passport, and I'll take my chances," I said.

But Harold shook his head, and both Mac and Miss Fallowfield cautioned against anything so precipitous. "There is still the operation to consider," she said.

"Let me guess: My uncle needs more money."

"Worse, he suspects that his identity has been discovered. It is fortunate the killer did not see that cigarette pack—or assumed that it was just ordinary tobacco."

"So you have Uncle Lastings's information," I said, annoyed that I was getting no credit for forcing myself to search poor Belinda's corpse. "You must already have what you need."

"What we have," said Miss Fallowfield, "is a desperate request for new documents."

"I hope you're quicker with his than you've been with mine."

This did not go over well. I got a lecture on patriotism and, more effective, Harold's threat to turn me over to the Kripos forthwith. Though I extracted such concessions as I could from them, come five o'clock, togged out and painted up, I arrived at the Eldorado. I hesitated in the doorway, undecided how best to enter. I felt miserable, totally down in the dumps, but wouldn't you know it, Dolly was always full of fun. Anything less tonight could suggest a dangerous foreknowledge, although the *Geschlossen* sign on the door could excuse a puzzled apprehension.

I settled on that, swung open the door, and pranced in. I waved to Herr K. and blew kisses to the rest of the girls, then stopped dead as if surprised. I actually was surprised. The reality had a different edge than even my most vivid imagining. Herr K. was up on a high ladder, hanging black bunting over the tops of the mirrors. "One of our own!" he wailed when he saw me. "One of our own has come to grief!"

The tables below, which should have been full of revelers in silk and pearls with dead birds in their hats, were occupied by various uniformed and plain-clothes officers. They were busy interviewing the staff, who were lined up along the rear bar, waiting their turns and whispering behind their fans. Half of the hostesses were wearing black so that, with their long legs and big faces, they looked like giant crows. An unpleasant effect, but I was mostly startled that the police were there so soon. Fortunately, I had the presence of mind to ask who had died.

"Belinda!" came the response from the bar, much to the annoyance of the detectives, who wanted to keep everything under control. Good luck with that at the Eldorado, the home of sexual anarchy! I saw at a glance that Belinda's death had caused genuine sorrow for some, sly satisfaction for others, but actual regret for all, because, as the staff complained in a shrill chorus, we would be closed for the whole night.

Shocking news all around! I managed to smear my eyeliner and eye shadow, and I made liberal use of my handkerchief. A good thing, too, because as a foreigner, I was already suspect, and my brief absence the previous night had been revealed and no doubt amplified. The hostesses were gossips, every one, and totally faithless. Where was the famed solidarity of the working classes with this lot?

I had more anxiety. My German, which is quite sufficient to order a meal, pick up a boy, or flirt at the coat-check counter, is not serviceable for anything complicated or serious. When it was my turn at the table, the young officer, very pale, very Norse, very straight—in every way, I guessed—knew no English. We struggled together for a while, with me inserting an English word whenever my German deserted me. Soon after I was dismissed, I was recalled for an older, English-speaking officer.

This one was wearing a mouse-colored topcoat over a tweed jacket and dark pants. He was plain of face, dark and bony with bags under his eyes, and tobacco on his breath—but I really do prefer older men, and he had the air of authority that I always find appealing. *Be careful, Francis!* The fact of the matter was that I was so nervous I was lured toward recklessness. "She was my friend," I said in English and put my hand on his knee. "A fine person. Her makeup was divine. And her dancing!" How thick could I lay it on? I was tempted to find out, but he was all business.

"You went out last night," he said, after consulting his notes. "At what time?"

I wiped my eyes, which really were streaming; the police favored a particularly vile brand of cigar, and the café was already toxic with smoke. I told him the time and wheezed enough to make my asthma attack plausible. I certainly needed fresh air right at that moment.

And what had I done?

"I took a walk and made a little purchase. For a coworker."

"A likely story," he said. His eyes were dark and intelligent. I reminded myself again to be careful.

"The dealer," I said, deciding to risk all, "is a perfect Apollo. You have to see him to believe him. I fancied my chances." I patted his knee for emphasis. If nothing else, I'd certainly learned to camp it up in Berlin.

"Doubtless I will see him." The detective's tone was heavy. "We will be checking your alibi. And your papers."

"The embassy has been helpful," I said. "My new passport is promised any day now."

"But you will not be leaving the city," the detective said. It was not a question.

"Certainly not!" I tried for indignation but just missed it. "Belinda was my friend. I'll do whatever I can to help." I wiped my eyes again, making a fine mess of my face so that when my interview was finished, I excused myself to visit the Eldorado WC—not the staff dump but the one for paying customers—to repair my makeup.

I was busy with my eyes—a little green, a little lavender—when Sabine came in. She leaned against one of the sinks and lit a cigarette. She was wearing a black-feathered hat that fit close to her head with a plume sticking up like a Valkyrie's helmet. Sabine favored dead white makeup à la the famous Anita Berger, plus maroon lipstick, eye shadow, and nail polish, none of which could diminish her large Roman nose and heavy brow ridge. Reflected in the mirror, she looked like a falcon on a bad night, but maybe my eye was influenced by the nastiness of the whole situation. Belinda's death changed the way I looked at everything.

"So," said Sabine. "The Queen is dead. *Long Live the Queen!* Isn't that what you English say?"

"We have a king at the moment."

"The treacherous cousin of our former Kaiser. That whole family is rotten to the core."

"Speak of your own royals. We have rather a better set." I'm hardly a monarchist, but Sabine put my hackles up. We weren't the ones who'd attacked Belgium, after all.

"Kings and all that: *kaput*," she said. Despite full drag, she was sounding less like Sabine and more like Sigi.

I shrugged. "Maybe this is not the night for politics."

She grabbed my arm. "Then why the hell did you mention Oskar's name?"

"Oskar? Who is this Oskar?"

"I heard you. 'A perfect Apollo.' They'll question him now."

"Too bad. I needed a witness. He was it. They won't arrest him over a few decks of snow."

Sabine drew on the cigarette and blew smoke in my face, then turned to check her makeup in the mirror. She was heavy-handed with the paints, and her features always resembled a mask. "It is not good to be known to the police." She met my eyes in the mirror and gave me a calculating look. "You admire Oskar?"

"Who wouldn't?"

"You must meet him, but outside working hours. Oskar is not really the Eldorado type."

This was an interesting development. Oskar looked like a prince, but instinct told me to stay away from Sabine.

"I'd like that. In happier times." I moved to leave the WC. We'd been told we could go once our interviews were over. I needed a drink, and I wanted out of Dolly's shoes.

Sabine put her hand on my arm again. "Sundays. We meet at the Zoo Station at nine A.M. and go for training out in the country. That's what Oskar likes."

What a ghastly prospect. I associate the countryside with pollen and animals and asthma attacks. The Germans seemed sold on cavorting in the open air, nude by preference, which did increase my interest. But was anyone, even the beautiful Oskar, worth the dreaded pine woods they went on about? "Fresh air and clean living?" I joked.

"The renewal of Germany depends on soil and blood," she said stiffly.

Some of Uncle Lastings's contacts had spouted a similar line. I thought that the last thing I wanted to do was to wander about the *Wald* with Sabine, especially Sabine in his Sigi mode. I was about to say something along those lines, to be Dolly and amusing and invent a fear of spiders or snakes.

Then I thought that, taken together with her comments in the taxi, Sabine's remarks might cast a different light altogether on Belinda's death. Could it really have been an inside job? Could one of the staff be the guilty party? And could I convince Mac and Harold that present danger required me to leave the Eldorado and get out of Berlin immediately? Perhaps via something clandestine, something that would be amusing later in a letter to Nan? It was worth a try.

"Thanks. I'll let you know," I said. "But I'm much too upset tonight to think straight. And the questioning! That detective with the piercing eyes—didn't he have me half-scared." I was about to add that I needed a drink, but suddenly I had a very strong urge to leave the premises—and definitely without Sabine's company.

CHAPTER TWELVE

Sometimes you're too clever by half, Francis. That's what Nan used to tell me, and I must admit that the night I returned from the Eldorado, full of ideas about why I should be whisked from Berlin to London, was one of those times. I mentioned Sabine's unexpected invitation to training in the country. "Sabine spouted off like one of Uncle Lastings's right-wing contacts," I told Miss Fallowfield. "She was jealous of Belinda and resented her as foreign competition."

Miss Fallowfield was skeptical. "This Sabine managed to shoot someone just off a busy street and dispose of the weapon in between dances?"

I didn't point out that was what the Kripos suspected I'd done. "I didn't mean she did it herself. I mean that she wouldn't have hesitated to point Belinda out to some fanatic. But I only know them from the Eldorado. Who else Belinda knew or who Sabine knows, all the rest of their lives, I have no idea."

"Now you have an opportunity to learn something about Sabine's life after hours, don't you?"

"Oh, no. Running around the Grünewald in lederhosen with flags and insignia? Not for me."

"If you are right, and you might be, you would be safest to feign an interest."

"I would be safest leaving the Eldorado and never going back."

"I'm not sure that's advisable." She drew me over to the window. "The police have followed you here. That's a sure sign of interest and most unfortunate."

"I had to give an address."

"Nonetheless, we will all be compromised if you should disappear. Flight suggests guilt. There would be serious questions."

"For you, not for me," I said. But without a passport or money or useful knowledge of border crossings, I was stuck. Instead of introducing me to the delights of nighttime Berlin, Uncle Lastings might better have coached me on evading passport controls and faking documents. I thought this over and sulked for a bit while Miss Fallowfield smoked impassively. Then I thought about Oskar. Could he possibly be detached from the excursion? Did my charm extend that far? It might be worth a try. "Sunday, I'll go as far as the station," I said, "and check the lay of the land."

"Excellent. Your uncle would be proud of you."

This was going too far. "My uncle would think I was a damn fool," I said, and I would have canceled the whole deal if she hadn't come up with money for a night out. I kicked off my heels, abandoned Dolly's frock and makeup and her ridiculous hat, put on my leather jacket, and set a course toward the Eldorado. There would be police in the area, but I took a circuitous route, and either I was lucky or the cops were taking shelter from the damp, because I found Oskar without being spotted.

The dealer was standing near a streetlight, his blond hair white-gold in the light and glistening with moisture from the mist that was rapidly turning to a cold rain. You can take my word for it, this romantic vision not only sent a little ripple of excitement to my nether regions, but also made me think that romping in the woods could not be all bad.

Nothing ventured, nothing gained, Francis. I strolled up and observed that it was a dark, raw night. He didn't seem to recognize me as a regular purchaser. That was good, as he had never shown the slightest interest in Dolly, the popular hatcheck girl.

"What'll you have?" he asked.

"I like champagne, myself."

"Expensive tastes." And he gave me a look. I hoped he liked what he saw; he really was breathtakingly handsome.

"Tonight I can indulge," I said, "provided I have company."

He looked around, but the few people about where huddled under umbrellas or scurrying for the nearest bar. Oskar turned up his collar against the drizzle and shrugged. "Nobody much buys on lousy nights."

"You'd think the public would need cheering up."

"You'd be wrong." He closed his satchel and slung it over his shoulder. "Lead on. Somewhere warm," he added. "I'm about frozen."

I knew a boy bar close by that fit the bill. The room was low and dark, with photos of boxers and football players and marchers with obscure flags and mysterious intentions, but the ceramic stove was big and hot and, despite the fog of coal smoke and cigarettes, both the wine and beer were good. Oskar found a place near the stove, and I set myself to be charming. It's not often that duty and pleasure coincide so neatly.

We had a bottle of wine and pea soup and sausages, two helpings each, and it was just a damn shame that Miss Fallowfield's largesse did not extend as far as a room, because a few moments in the alley, clothes rumpled, cold hands on hot skin, an ecstatic wrestle against the bricks, could not quite erase the discomfort of rain above, garbage below, and slime underfoot. I don't mind squalor and I adore risk, but even Apollo loses a little when speed is a necessity and cold water is running down my neck.

Oscar was maybe thinking along the same lines because, walking to the tram stop, he said, "A gang of us are going out to the Grünewald on Sunday. A bit of hiking, maybe some music. Why don't you come?"

"I'd like that," I said. "Though I'm not so good at hiking." I tapped my chest. Asthma might not be a strong enough excuse, but consumption was still common in Berlin.

"We don't have to walk the whole way. The forest is truly lovely."

"All right." I put my arms around him and kissed him. He really had the most beautiful round backside, and he smelled of smoke and sausages and the fine camel hair of his old coat. Oskar was a professor's son who had known better days with a nice wardrobe, a future, and respectability. Maybe not the package for my deepest, darkest tastes, which I was slowly coming to understand, but his eyes were a gorgeous blue, and he had strong, even features and a mouth so crisply defined that it might have been carved. Plus he was blond. I suspected that blonds might be my weakness.

"Sunday," he called as he stepped onto the tram.

"Sunday it is!" I walked home, fizzy with lust and light of heart, until I spotted someone loitering near the front of our building. Could he be *loitering with intent*, as Nan's crime stories so often had it? Maybe. Or a Kripo plainclothesman? Or one of the street fighters who had visited me at Fritz's? I was accumulating possibilities at an alarming rate.

Over on the darker side of the street, I walked straight past Miss Fallowfield's. At the next side street, I risked a look. He was still loitering with a vengeance, the smoke of his pipe mixing with the fog. I went three blocks out of my way, crossed the street again, and took a circuitous route to the back of Miss Fallowfield's building. I hoped that no one was watching there, as I didn't fancy a rough night's sleep. But either I'd been needlessly alarmed or the spies were lazy. No one saw me squeeze past the alley garbage cans and scramble over the rickety wall into what had once been the garden.

With the townhouse's conversion into flats, this space was now taken up with several WCs of an unwholesome character, Miss Fallowfield having secured the only indoor plumbing in the building. And wouldn't you know it, I had no sooner begun wading through the weeds and nettles that edged the wall than I heard one of the WC doors open. I froze against the wall.

"That you, Hermann?" a woman called in German. She sounded anxious, and she had a flashlight. I hoped that she would not think to run it along the wall, because one good shriek could alert the whole building. Then something moved farther down the yard. It was one of the large skinny cats that haunted the neighborhood, and for once the animal kingdom was on my side. Satisfied about the source of the noise, the woman went into the WC and closed the door.

And kept it closed. Was she ill? A closet smoker? A consumer of illicit drugs or dirty magazines? While I stood in the drizzle, she could have knocked off a few chapters of *War and Peace*. I was nearly soaked through before I heard the door open and saw a dim figure moving back toward the building.

Dazed by nicotine or some other potion, might she leave the house unlocked? I gave the door a try, but such carelessness was too much to expect. Berliners had learned caution where personal security was concerned. No, my only hope looked to be the fire escape, a rusty contraption that ran straight past Miss Fallowfield's flat. She kept a couple of pots of geraniums on the landing.

The trick would be to get up to where the steps started, and that meant pulling down the ladder that allowed access to the ground. The last rung was well above my head. At school I used to cut gym class whenever I could and, doubtless as a consequence, my vertical jump was disappointing. When I failed to reach the ladder after several tries, I climbed back over the wall and hoisted the least full of the garbage cans into the garden. Once the can was under the ladder, I clambered onto the top and, with the extra height and a great feat of balance, managed to get my hands around the last rung. I gave a tug and nearly lost my footing. Gave another and got a handful of rust. Finally, clutching the rung, I jumped off the garbage can.

The ladder rattled down. Nicely done, if I hadn't awakened the whole building. I dragged the garbage can back to the wall and returned it to the alley—not exactly a silent job, either. I waited for a few moments in the dark garden, but apparently no one was curious enough to investigate. I climbed to the first level and hauled the ladder up after me, an operation that made a fine screech and just about took my arms from their sockets. I'd really expected better from German manufacturing, and figuring that half the building's tenants would be at their windows, I crouched on the wet iron grate of the fire escape.

A third-floor window opened, a scare that nearly launched me into wheezing. After a moment, the sash closed, but I waited some more, figuring I could hardly be any wetter. When there were no other sounds except the pattering rain and a distant train whistle, I edged past two windows, one partly open, and made my way up to the second story where a little glimmer of light ran between the heavy drapes of one room. I tapped on the glass and waited. Tapped again, harder. I was about to call out, when the drapes parted. Miss Fallowfield stood holding a revolver that looked a good deal like Uncle Lastings's Webley. She set it down when she saw me and lifted the sash.

"What on earth are you doing?" She did not seem impressed by my initiative, and I sensed that she was sorry I had seen the revolver.

"There was a man outside."

"No matter. Didn't he see you leave earlier?"

"No, he wasn't there when I left. The police must have been satisfied that I'd given the proper address." Uninvited, I sat down in one of her big armchairs. I was cold, wet, and tired, and my hands were full of little pieces of rusted iron.

"Possibly," she said and added in a more conciliatory tone. "Very good, Francis." More to the point, she poured me a decent tot of her good whiskey. "And your Sunday excursion? Is that still on?"

"Very much so," I said and winked. Let her think that over!

• • •

Sunday was fine. The cold rain off the Baltic had disappeared, and the Grünewald sounded lovely—if you had a taste for trees. I didn't, but the moment I saw Oskar lounging at the station with his comrades, I knew that I would go, even if I got a smirk from Sigi and many sly references to the charms of the new hatcheck girl. I just closed my ears, because if ever there was a boy built for lederhosen, it was Oskar.

In their gray-green shirts and shorts and patterned neckerchiefs, Sigi and the others looked like the pupils of some horrid physical culture class. But even in short pants and what looked to be a combat league shirt, Oskar was still a prince. I had to keep myself from throwing my arms around his neck. *Easy, Francis!*

Onto the train and off to the woods. Jolly singing seemed to be on the program and, as threatened, one of the comrades was carrying a violin. The railroad conductors prevented an impromptu concert on the train, but when we reached the woods, music broke out, aided and abetted by other youth group comrades. One squad provided a drum, and another had a member packing a trumpet. Once we were assembled, a good few dozen strong, the plan was a vigorous march down a track in the Grünewald, violin squawking, drum thumping, and trumpet heralding our every step.

The only songs I know are "God Save the Queen," which I thought unsuitable in present company, and "Watch on the Rhine," which I know by heart and in tune, thanks to gloomy hours listening to Fritz's father. My efforts at this were appreciated, and we stamped along hollering and working up a thirst all the way to a little tavern, which I suspected had been the destination all along. Beer, black bread, cheese, and wurst. All good, while the fiddle and the trumpet took turns amusing the patrons and were successful enough to pay for our meal. The German passion for music is one of many mysteries, along with their appetite for marching in the woods.

After this welcome break, the plan was for the keener members to engage in what Heinz, who seemed to be the leader of the outfit, called military preparedness. As far as I could see, this was going to consist of clambering over rocks and fallen trees while carrying the wooden rifles that had appeared from the back of the tavern. There would be military marching drills, and I believe that something with mock bayonets was to be what Uncle Lastings would call the *pièce de résistance*. Thank you, Uncle Lastings.

I was afraid that Oskar might be tempted by these delights, but when the others assembled, he waved them off. He wanted another beer, he said, and he would keep me company since I was not physically fit. A humiliating reason, and I was almost vain enough to say, "Let's go. I'll be fine." Almost, but not quite. At the very least, I expected sniggers and complaints and heavy teasing, but they accepted this without question. Beauty as spectacular as Oskar's apparently has its privileges.

We sat and drank in the now quiet tavern, then strolled down an overgrown road toward the river dotted, that afternoon, with rowing shells and sailboats. We stopped in a little glade out of sight of the track. The grass had dried after the rain, and the sun through the trees dappled Oskar's pale, strong body with shade. I would take a hike anytime if he was at the end of it. He liked lying nude in the sun, and afterward we put on our pants and walked shirtless into a little meadow. Some people were sunbathing, more or less naked, and others were doing gymnastics, turning cartwheels and backflips and trying to walk on their hands.

We sat down where we could see the water, and Oskar lit a cigarette.

"You're right," I said. "The Grünewald is lovely." Of course, I meant present company, but he did make the otherwise hostile greenery tolerable.

"You are very nice," he said. Oskar was well educated, and I think that my ungrammatical and profane German maybe offended him, because he preferred to speak in English. "It is too bad you have no taste for the military life."

"I saw enough of military life," I said, forgetting momentarily that Francis Wood's father would not necessarily have been a cavalry officer and a Boer War vet. He might have been something quite nice—maybe a sworn pacifist with no blood lust whatsoever. "My father was very big on fitness and readiness."

"It's a good thing. Prussia grew from blood and iron, and what Germany needs is a rebuilt *Reichswehr*."

"Not for a while, though," I said. "Not with the treaty."

"No," he said, and his face darkened.

I admitted that they had gotten the worst of things, but they conveniently forgot their crazy Kaiser and attacking Belgium and their treaty with Russia.

"But that will change," he continued in his correct and careful English. "The youth of Germany are preparing. We will rebuild our country. We will have a revolution."

"I thought you already had one."

"A milk-and-water deal," he said. "We have other plans."

I didn't take this too seriously, in spite of Belinda and Uncle Lastings and the embassy people. Every bar had its resident politicians and, although it might just have been my uncertain German, it seemed that every other chap had links to one of the conspiracies of the moment.

I preferred to lie in the sun and admire Oskar, who even smoked elegantly. I believe I said something along those lines, because he looked at me quite seriously, head up and wreathed in smoke. "It is too bad that this will all soon be over," he said.

"What do you mean?"

"There will be no place for you in the new Germany to come."

"Well, I didn't expect that you'd be recruiting Irishmen," I said, although I guessed that was not what he meant. To be honest, I was a bit shocked.

"I mean this," he said, and he put his hand on my shoulder.

"You can't change your nature with a uniform. You may get your revolution, but you'll still be the same. With the same desires."

"You're dead wrong there," Oskar said coldly. "I'll be a soldier in the new Germany and a different person altogether."

I heard Nan in my ear say, *The leopard cannot change its spots.* That was one old saw I thought better not to mention, because Oskar, clever as he was, struck me as naive and a bit desperate. "Soldiers," I said, thinking of Uncle Lastings and Belinda, too, "are sometimes queer. Guns don't care and horses don't, either."

"That is the British army," he said in a superior way, and I think that I might have been forced into defending that deeply hostile organization if we hadn't heard the thump of the drum and our returning comrades.

CHAPTER THIRTEEN

The sun was still as bright on the Havel, the mood of the gang as cheerful, a last beer at the tavern as good, but the day was spoiled for me. I decided to leave at the first stop in Berlin and have no more to do with Oskar or his friends, a ridiculous bunch of boy scouts. Residents of liberated Berlin, no less! I was silent and gloomy all the way back to the city, and Oskar picked up on that, because although I left the train without saying good-bye, he jumped off after me.

"Francis, wait!"

"Fuck you, Oskar."

He followed when I ran down the stairs and caught my arm. "You are misunderstanding me," he said. "You are not native here and you are owed a warning."

"Thanks a lot. But while you're playing soldier and dreaming up a greater Germany, I want to live now. As I am."

His face looked sad. "We are not playing. We are dead earnest. I want to help my country, and for that I must be a soldier."

"Sure, be a soldier. Back to the trenches! Fine, I'm all for it.

But you really want to be a *normal* soldier, don't you? Whatever normal is. Do you think you can change your ways with a uniform?" I was angry; I saw how unhappy he was, standing there handsome, clever, and educated. *Why do we make ourselves miserable*, I wondered, and in the emotion of the moment, I said, "Listen, I have a soldier uncle, front line, decorated from here to there. He sleeps with boys and never gives it a thought. Now that's a good soldier in my book."

Oskar's face changed slightly. "We are different," he said. "You English . . ."

If I hadn't been at sixes and sevens between lust and anger, I'd have noticed the change in his expression. Instead, I told him to remember that I was really Irish and that if he was going to start in about the Prussian army and the sacred soil of the Fatherland again, I'd say *auf Wiedersehen*. I headed for where I thought a tram stop might be and, mind in a whirl, I almost ran into a couple of men who stepped from a *Lokal* carrying heavy walking sticks. They had caps pulled low over their eyes and matching brown shirts under their jackets.

"*Verzeihung*," I muttered. As I moved to go past, I heard Oskar shout, "Run, Francis!"

I looked back. His face was white, and his hands were in fists. One of the men blocked my path with his cudgel-size stick, and his companion leaped toward Oskar with his weapon raised. "Traitors to the Fatherland!" the man shouted and brought the stick down full force. Oscar dodged to one side but was struck on his right shoulder. He let out a shriek, and his assailant backhanded the weapon against his thigh.

"Hey!" I cried and, without thinking, snatched the cane that was blocking my path. "We are not armed!"

This appeal to good sportsmanship must have surprised the fighter, because I got a good grip on his weapon. He was taller and heavier, but I held on until he jerked me across the sidewalk and brought me to one knee. Without shaking me off, he could not go to his companion's assistance, which might be needed, for in desperation, Oskar had picked up one of the municipal litter cans, a sturdy iron basket that he swung before his face as a shield. I heard a thump and a bang as the cane landed on the basket, then a pop as it got caught between the iron bands and snapped.

Instantly, Oskar's assailant dropped the cane and lunged at him with his fists, only to be struck by the heavy can and dropped onto the sidewalk. Angered, his big friend wrenched the cane from my hands and turned to deal with Oskar. I grabbed for his legs, then struggled to get onto his back and put my hands around his neck. We lurched back and forth across the sidewalk before I was dumped onto the pavement along with the cane, which rolled into the gutter.

Perhaps Oskar thought that we had reached a stalemate or, perhaps, with his injured shoulder, the can was too heavy for him to hold, because he had already dropped it when the second fighter closed in on him. This one was clearly confident with his fists, and though Oskar was quick, I could see that he was not nearly as skillful. Hampered by his shoulder and the blow to his thigh, he could not evade the quick flurry of blows that swelled one eye and opened his lip. The fighter grabbed the front of his shirt and seemed determined to beat him to the ground.

I scrambled to my feet, avoided the man still groaning on the pavement, and snatched the shattered end of his cane. Remembering my success with the bayonet, I thrust it as hard as I could into the fighter's back. Despite a heavy leather jacket, he gave a grunt and released Oskar.

"Run, Francis!" Oskar took off, half-stumbling, blood streaming from his face.

This time I didn't hesitate, especially since other brown-shirted figures were emerging from the bar. Despite his injuries, Oskar was soon ahead of me, and though he kept looking back and calling encouragement, I was falling behind when we saw a tram approaching. A last dash over the tracks to the platform and into the car left the fastest of our pursuers thumping their fists against the closing door and sending us off with a stream of obscenities. The tram slid away, and, relieved, I took a huge breath and felt my lungs contract. The car went black and red before I could manage some air, and I was gasping so much that Oskar had to pay our fares.

We must have looked like a pair of street toughs, and, thinking back, it was a surprise we were allowed on. But then people were used to beggars and mutilated vets and brawls in the streets. Especially around election time, political differences tended to be settled with fists. I propped myself up against a pole in the tram and looked back. Far down the line, a group of men in brown shirts were clustered on the platform. Our attackers.

As soon as I could speak, I asked, "Who were they?"

Oskar shook his head. He'd wiped off the worst of the blood with his handkerchief, but his mouth was cut, one side of his face was swollen, and he'd have a black eye for sure. He kept massaging his injured leg and trying to flex his bruised shoulder. "SA. The Brownshirts."

"Bolshies?"

"No Reds in this area. They're Röhm's men." When he could see this meant nothing, he added, "NSDAP. The Nazis. Ever since Goebbels, their new gauleiter, arrived, they treat anyone with a different opinion as the enemy. They're mostly drunks out for a fight."

"I can see that." I felt as if I'd been wrestling cement. But Goebbels . . . Wasn't that Uncle Lastings's supposed pigeon? And NSDAP—that, too, rang a bell. "Didn't they try to overthrow the government?"

"Right. The *Hitlerputsch* in '23. They wanted to take over Bavaria. They are a political outfit now."

Not entirely, I thought, *if they are buying weapons through my uncle*. I sincerely hoped that Lastings had cheated them. And that he was steering well clear of their street fighters.

"I would have been badly hurt without you, Francis. I am sincerely in your debt."

Something about his careful, almost schoolboy English touched me. "You told me to run." He would have taken them on alone and kept me safe. He was a prince, and I patted his uninjured shoulder. "I think we are even," I said. I meant that the unpleasantness of the afternoon was erased, forgotten. That I could ignore his odd politics. That I still thought he was marvelous.

"But you have deceived me," he said and gave me a look that I probably should have considered more carefully. "You have had some military training." And he mimed a bayonet thrust.

"Strictly observation." This was not the time to brag of my unsuspected skill. "I told you I've seen enough soldiering. And soldiers."

"That may be so, but it saved your life," he said, "and maybe mine."

We got out at the next stop. Oskar had stiffened during the ride, and he hobbled off painfully. It was clear that he needed some care and cleaning up, but Miss Fallowfield's was out of the question. While she would doubtless be interested in my outing and its conclusion, I didn't need to be told that her house was verboten. I said that my landlady was peculiar and asked if he couldn't go home.

"I can't go home in this state," he said, and added that his parents did not approve of his life.

I understood about that! "The stork sometimes bollocks up its deliveries," I said.

Oskar gave a bitter laugh and suggested his *Lokal*. We hopped a tram on another line to the bar. When we limped inside, his arm around my shoulders, blood on his shirt, and his face swollen, he was greeted like a returning warrior, and some of his heroic glow was cast on yours truly.

Most of the gang from the Grünewald outing were present, including Sigi, who sniggered in the corner and whispered about Dolly. I could ignore him, for while Oskar was washed and bandaged and his bruises treated, I had glasses of beer and schnapps on the house. If Sigi was envious or jealous or suspicious, the rest were enthusiastic. I had helped the popular Oskar on a day of combat, so I was thumped on the back and almost forgiven for being English. The whole evening became so jolly that I put aside Oskar's warning. If the thought crossed my mind that I had probably been indiscreet, I refused to blame myself.

My whole predicament was the fault of the security people, and when Miss Fallowfield asked me how things had gone, I gave her an edited version. Given that the right-wing fighters were at odds with one another as well as with the Reds, I believed that Oskar's friends had enough to occupy their minds. I told myself that it was unlikely anyone would be suspicious of Dolly. I reminded myself of that at least once every night, for the atmosphere at the Eldorado had grown poisonous.

Sabine was now the Queen of the Dance Floor, but like everyone else, she was on edge, which made me doubt that she'd had anything to do with Belinda's death. We were all so suspicious and nervous that we took to saying "keep safe" instead of "good night" when we left. That was one thing. The other was that my trip with the sports group had attached Sabine to me more firmly than ever. Dolly really had to get a move on to avoid sharing taxis, because Sabine liked to bore me with her conquests of the evening and with Sigi's plans for military preparedness and general fitness.

The rides were so tiresome, I suspected that Sabine just wanted to keep an eye on me. She also liked to mention that I had gone out on the evening Belinda was killed and, rather inconsistently, to commiserate with me for "losing my special friend." I really wanted to tell both Sabine and Sigi to fuck off, but that would have been stupid. Miss Fallowfield was right; I was safest hiding in plain sight as the jolly English hatcheck girl with the delightfully profane and fractured German.

So long as Dolly was firmly in everyone's mind, I didn't believe that Francis Wood, her alter ego, would be connected with that other Francis, the accessory to murder who had a spy for an uncle and who, against all expectations and very long odds, had not only escaped an attack, but injured a former member of the Freikorps. That's what I told myself, but the real reason I did not relay my suspicions to Miss Fallowfield, Mac, and Harold was that I liked Oskar better than anyone else I'd met in Berlin. Now that we were "brothers in the struggle" and a lot of other things I didn't take seriously, it seemed a good idea to keep seeing him.

Besides, I certainly agreed with Uncle Lastings that it was foolish to let anxiety stand in the way of pleasure. Beyond pretending that my German was worse than it really was, I took no other precautions, and I saw Oskar just about every day. Quite often at night, I'd slip out to buy Martha her "pick-me-up" and take a few more minutes off the clock with him. There were no more street fights, no more alarms, no more bodies in the alley. Except for Dolly's damn heeled shoes, I was enjoying Berlin mostly at His Majesty's government's expense. How many people could say that?

So a week later, when Oskar said "We're going to the island this weekend. Call in sick at the club," I was seriously tempted.

"Somewhere in the Grünewald?" I asked.

"No, up north. It's a Baltic island. Very wild and beautiful. Deserted beaches, woods." He raised a flirtatious eyebrow. His face had just about healed, and the dark bruises had faded to a faint greenish tinge.

I regretted that I couldn't afford such a long train ride.

"My treat," said Oskar. "We're assembling at the Forester at nine o'clock. It's a *Lokal* near the station."

"Why don't I meet you at the train?" I felt I saw quite enough of Sigi in his role as Queen of the Eldorado, and I didn't share the gang's enthusiasm for marching through the streets.

"If we get the tickets ahead of time, we get a group discount," Oskar said. "Do come. It'll be nice to have someone intelligent to talk to."

How could I resist?

Dear Nan,

I am off to see Rügen Island on the wild Baltic coast with some friends. Don't be surprised if I come home speaking fluent German, as these are all boys my own age. The sea air should be good for my asthma, too, so you don't have to worry about me. But do keep sending all mail to Francis Wood. I'll explain about that when I see you next. Hope you've gotten a job—and a nice one, too. Mine is all right, but I feel I need a little vacation. . . .

The next morning, I dropped the letter in the mail on the way out and left with a light heart. I'd decided that when I returned, I was going to tell Miss Fallowfield that I was done with Dolly and the Eldorado, that one way or another I intended to go home. *You have to stand up for yourself, Francis,* Nan said in my ear, and as I headed for the train, I thought that's just what I would do.

CHAPTER FOURTEEN

I skipped the Forester and went straight to the train station. Running around in the woods with Oskar's friends was one thing. A public parade with would-be soldiers, especially German would-be soldiers, was quite another. Without being overly staunch about king and country, I have my standards. I found the platform for trains to Stralsund, the closest mainland stop, bought a wurst sandwich, and sat down to wait. About 9:30, the gang arrived, all togged out in gray-green shirts, lederhosen, and hiking boots.

"Francis!" Oskar called, all smiles. "We thought you left us!"

"I got delayed," I said, throwing my arm across his shoulders. "I thought I might miss you if I went to the *Lokal*."

"No matter, you are here," he said and handed me a ticket.

Sigi gave a curt nod and didn't say anything. Odd that someone so chatty in drag should be so laconic in pants, even in embarrassingly short pants, but I sensed that he was not pleased. Not pleased that I was coming on the excursion? Or not pleased that I had gone directly to the station? His problem in either case.

I sat next to Oskar in our third-class carriage, and as we rattled out of Berlin, he outlined the program. A visit to the beach
at Putbus, still out of season but scenic with sand dunes and
quiet, secluded beaches along the Baltic. I quite liked the sound
of that, I told him, and made him laugh. Oskar had a wonderful laugh, too seldom heard, and he dropped his hand onto my
knee and promised that we'd have a good time. After a night in
a hostel, we were in for a bicycling trip to the chalk cliffs. "Very
steep, very white."

"Chalk? Like Dover?"

"Yes, but I think higher. We'll have a picnic and cycle back.
We have a friend with a big house near the station. We'll stay
there and visit the beach. Monday night you are all better and
back at the hatcheck counter. Great, right?"

I could think of a few things about the itinerary that were not
great, starting with what sounded like a long bike ride.

"But you cycle, don't you, Francis? People cycle in England?"

"Sure," I said. "I've been on a bike." Nan taught me as a child.
I had a memory of her putting her left foot on the pedal and
swinging her right, skirt and all, over the seat and pushing off.
It's easy enough, Francis, she said, and I soon got the hang of it.
Both at home and at school, bikes of one sort or another became
my getaway vehicles. But those had been short runs, away from
the stable yard or out of sight of the rugby pitch. This promised
to be something quite different.

We reached Putbus in midafternoon for *Wehrsport* training
on the beach. Translation: running around in the heavy sand and
hurdling a series of improvised obstacles. I lay in the dunes and

stared at the sky. Sigi felt that this showed a lack of pluck and spirit and tried to provoke me. Good luck with that, Sigi! I could turn a deaf ear, because everyone knew I'd come through for Oskar in his moment of need.

"Straight arm thrust! Perfect bayonet form. No hesitation!" That was Oskar at his *Lokal* once he was bandaged up. "You might have shouted, Francis, but I'm telling you he was perfect!"

After that endorsement, anything else I attempted in the military line was sure to fall short. I told Sigi I was saving my breath and energy for other things, and when Oskar took a break from mock soldiering, I was rewarded. I was still skeptical of beaches, but I thought much better of sand dunes.

So all was good—the floor of the hostel hard but clean, the weather the next morning perfect: blue sky, mild breeze, and sea light. Even the long ride through farm country and the beech woods to the cliffs was not as bad as it might have been. The sea breeze swept away the dust and pollen, and we went at a leisurely pace, for Oskar seemed rather subdued. It was Sigi—not Oskar—who shouted for impromptu races along the road or demanded breaks for calisthenics. As the day went on, I increasingly had the feeling that the youth group was paling on Oskar, but perhaps he was just missing his family and home, where I understood that the remnants of a comfortable life still existed. He had apparently not returned to their flat since the fight.

"Where have you been staying?" I asked, thinking how nice it would have been if only Miss Fallowfield had been a tolerant Berlin landlady, instead of someone with ties to His Majesty's government.

"Here and there. With Sigi, mostly."

That, no doubt, accounted for his growing lack of enthusiasm for the group. "Sigi is very keen," I said, by which I meant a fanatical idiot.

"Sigi is ambitious." Oscar looked over his shoulder and checked that all the other cyclists were ahead of us. "He tires of the youth group. I think he may join the SA."

"The men who attacked you! What can he be thinking?"

Oskar shrugged. "He has friends. Some people he met at the Eldorado."

"Really!" I was surprised in spite of the fact that, like Sigi, Belinda had been seriously political and that my rascally and complicated uncle enjoyed the club as well. I couldn't help thinking of the Eldorado as a place for frivolity, for sex and make-believe, even though my own role there was deceptive, and I had a hidden agenda.

"They are encouraging him," Oskar continued. "Sigi wants a fight. He wants a revolution or a putsch, and he thinks the SA will lead one."

"Good riddance," I said, feeling uneasy. I was sure now that Sigi in his Sabine duds had been keeping an eye on me at the club. But I had no idea why he would be eager for me to join the youth group if he was leaving himself. One thing I did know: Cycling to the back of beyond to visit steep and magnificent cliffs was damned foolish when no one in Berlin knew where I was. I should have stayed home and reported for work at the Eldorado.

You can bet that I was on high alert for the rest of the day, especially when we descended to the beach via some rickety wooden stairs. Above us, the cliffs loomed spectrally white against the blue sky and some dark clouds drifting further out over the Baltic. At the water's edge, the scene was dramatic and faintly sinister with the narrow, deserted beach backed by forest-topped cliffs. We took off our boots and shoes and stuck our feet in the cold Baltic water then lay about on the sand and listened to the light surf rolling the stones near the edge. The boys smoked and talked politics, their German often too rapid and specialized for me to follow. I watched the clouds and kept a close eye on Sigi.

I'd expected a bit of argy-bargy from him, but except for the usual remarks about Dolly, he ignored me. I began to think that I was wrong, a conviction that grew after he proposed a race back up the stairs. When I offered to go up first to time their arrival, he gave me his watch without hesitation. "Good idea," he said. "You're never going to make commando."

Too right! I stood at the top, watched them charge up, straining their legs and losing their breath, and called out their times. Then, apparently satisfied that they had exerted themselves sufficiently for the Fatherland, we cycled back past Putbus to a hamlet near the rail bridge to the mainland. I had expected something along the lines of the hostel or—death to my lungs—a hay barn. Instead, we rolled up to a dark, imposing brick house with a steep German-style roof of red tiles. It sat in a grove of conifers, and I could see a variety of outbuildings behind. Except for the architectural style, the house reminded me of a prosperous country house in Ireland.

The master of this estate was the friend Oskar had mentioned, Oberst Kurt Weick, a tall, thin man with gray hair and dueling

scars on his angular face. He was a very Prussian officer, still with
perfect military posture despite a false forearm adjusted at the
proper angle to hold his cigarette. To smoke, he had to lift his
arm from his shoulder, which gave him an oddly mechanical air,
as if he were as much machine as man, an impression strength-
ened by his small, chilly gray eyes, set in a permanent squint
against the smoke. There was something far away in them, as if
his vision were permanently fixed on some point in no-man's-
land just beyond his trenches.

When Oskar mentioned that I was a foreign friend of the
group, he welcomed me to the house in near perfect English. As
a friend of Oskar's, I was very welcome, he told me. He clearly
knew most of the other boys, and I understood that what he
referred to as *der Bund* was in some way under his patronage.
At a word from him, they all snapped to attention and marched
smartly into the house. Of course, in this company, I was a complete slacker, but military discipline was even further from my
mind than usual, for I had the disturbing notion that I had seen
him before.

Yes, I was sure. The arm alone was unmistakable, and I am
rarely wrong about a face. His pallid map of bony angles and
scars was memorable, and as I passed him and entered the house,
I noticed that he had one glass eye. Where had I seen this appari-
tion? On the S-Bahn, in the street? I thought not. In my mind's
eye, I saw a homburg, a fine dark coat, a silk tie, a single leather
glove. The homburg did it. I had taken it in at the hatcheck
counter at the Eldorado. I was sure of it. He'd visited the club,
although he wasn't one of our regulars. Just a casual patron out

for the sights of decadent Berlin or a Prussian officer with a secret yen for silks and feathers? Or was he the one who was "encouraging" Sigi to hope for a brown shirt and street violence?

"*Beeile dich, Francis.*" Sigi was standing halfway up the staircase leading from a dark paneled foyer crowded with mounted antlers like branches of bones.

"*Ja, ja.*" Up a second stair, we reached a vast attic set up with camp beds. Oskar had already grabbed two by a low semicircular window, and he patted the one next to him. Delightful idea, but even Oskar couldn't distract me from the thought that three of us from the Eldorado was too much of a coincidence. I was already wondering if I could possibly leave undetected and how I would get off the island if I did.

But first we had dinner, laid out in a banquet-size dining room. We sat on benches at a long trestle table. The floor was stone, the walls white-washed brick, the decor more antlers. Somewhere, the oberst's ancestors must have shot a powerful number of stags. Everything from the furniture to the massive fireplace was plain and functional like the fittings of a military barracks, but the food was good—the first real beef I'd had since the Adlon. The hotel's lavish restaurant with its soft-footed waiters, silver trays, and covered dishes seemed an age away, and yet my visit with Uncle Lastings had led to everything that had happened since. Perhaps even to this dinner, an idea that gave me pause.

There were toasts with steins of beer and bursts of military and patriotic song. I alternately watched Sigi and Oberst Weick. Sigi was very active, always the first with a toast or a song. He wanted desperately to be noticed, but the colonel was not really interested in him. Instead, Weick's eyes strayed to Oskar, a bias that was completely understandable. Oskar was beautiful and fit, with a natural dignity. *One of nature's bloody aristocrats* is what Uncle Lastings would have said, another unexpectedly useful category.

I followed his glance and smiled at my friend, but out of the corner of my eye I saw that Weick was also watching me, the stranger in his house. Had he noticed my overwhelming attractions? Probably not when Oskar was sitting beside me, but he was interested. For although I told myself it was just my imagination, whenever I glanced in Weick's direction, I met his chilly eyes—both real and glass—focusing on me.

When dinner was over, I asked Oskar if he thought that we might ask to see the grounds. "We need to walk off that splendid dinner," I said to Oberst Weick, when we approached him.

"Of course." He made a gracious gesture, turned mechanical by his false hand and forearm. "You can see Stralsund from the headland. Perhaps others will wish some exercise?"

But they wished to sit before the fire and worship at his feet. I had the feeling that there would be war stories, possibly maps, certainly an exchange of political hopes and fears, and complaints. Awkward for one of the erstwhile Allies!

"We will not be long," Oskar said. He had picked up on the atmosphere, but he did not want to seem unappreciative. There are some serious disadvantages to nice manners. Once outside, he lit a cigarette. Although our host was a chain smoker, he did not approve of the boys smoking while "in training."

"Do you know the oberst?" I asked as we crossed the gravel drive in the long northern twilight.

"Not well. I've only met him a couple of times before. He is a distant relative of Sigi's, I think."

"Really."

There was a long pause during which I debated how candid I should be. We'd come within sight of the stables, beautifully built but smelling all too strongly of horse, before I said, "Do you trust him? And Sigi?"

Oskar gave me a look.

"I feel I should leave," I said. "I feel I should leave tonight."

"Without telling the group, you mean?"

"That's what I have in mind."

I'd half-expected Oskar to laugh and tell me that I was imagining things. Instead, he said, "Sigi doesn't like you, but you are quite safe. With me and the others."

"And the oberst?"

"I know nothing bad of him. He makes you uncomfortable?"

I shrugged. Oskar was a patriot awaiting the resurgence of his country. This was not the moment to discuss Uncle Lastings or the mess he'd left me. "Perhaps it is just his injuries and that mechanical arm."

"We are used to such," Oskar said in a heavy tone of voice and threw away the butt of his cigarette.

At the edge of the lawn, we could see the water and the rail bridge. Distance contracted the span, but it still looked tricky and dangerous.

"Come back inside. It would be rude to leave now," Oskar said, putting his arm around my shoulders and leaning his head against mine.

I was really very fond of him, and I let myself be persuaded that my reservations about Sigi and our host were an unbecoming timidity. Usually, when I am accused of cowardice, it means I'm in for something unpleasant, but I put this wisdom aside, thinking that I might slip away later if either Sigi or the oberst did anything to *put the wind up*, as Uncle Lastings would say. And, admittedly, inside I found that all was harmonious. Literally.

We had another round of beer and singing before the fireplace, accompanied by an accordion that the oberst must have kept for just such occasions. One of the boys played quite well, mostly marches and patriotic numbers that got the group singing and stamping their feet in unison, but a few dance tunes, too, so that the company was up and hopping, boots clattering on the stone floor, shouts ringing off the high timber ceiling. I flirted with Oskar and kept a weather eye on Weick.

Eventually, the group ran out of energy. Cycling, calisthenics, races, and the oberst's beer had worn us out; the party broke up. We said *Gute Nacht* and *dankeschön* to our host and climbed the two flights to the loft. Upstairs, I glanced through the windows. The moon was down; the fields, black; the Baltic, a distant sliver of gray; the town on the far shore, reduced to a few tiny pricks of light. Walking to the bridge in pitch-darkness did not seem like such an attractive idea. I lay down on my cot, put my coat under my head, and pulled up the blanket. I'd had just enough of boarding-school dormitories to acquire a knack for falling asleep amid the snores and farts and giggles of other boys. I was gone almost instantly, and the light was gray in the low windows when I next raised my head.

Two lines of cots with sleepers rolled in their blankets against the morning chill. A bird singing. The rustle of something exploring the attic wall—country houses all have mice. Unless they have rats. I sat up. No one moved. I looked over at Oskar's cot and my heart jumped. Empty. Of course, he'd gone looking for a chamber pot or made the trek downstairs to the WC. The oberst had been generous with the beer, and it would be a good idea if I made the same trip.

I stood up in my underwear and felt around for my shoes. I saw that Oskar's were gone. And his pants. Proper German courtesy? Do not wander down to use your host's WC in your underwear? I'd like to think so. I located my pants and put them on. Also my shirt, as I noticed that Oskar's was gone, too. And his sweater. Did he need a sweater to visit the WC? I pulled on mine anyway. Then, carrying my shoes, I crossed the attic to the door and the stairs, reminding myself not to hurry and to gently ease the door open. Then downstairs. What time was it? Having gone to bed so much earlier than usual, I had no idea. Maybe three? Maybe four? I returned from the Eldorado in the wee hours and woke when the sun was high.

The hall and stairs on the second floor had a carpet runner. I put on my shoes but walked carefully, listening for running water, the sounds of Oskar in the WC, a quiet and private place with possibilities. Which one was the door? It wouldn't do to open the oberst's room, no indeed. I stood in the hall for what felt like a quarter of an hour with an impatient bladder and a growing anxiety. Oskar was clearly not using our host's facilities, and I decided not to go looking, either.

Down the main stairs, past the antler forest of dead stags, to the big oak door. In the dark foyer, I felt for the bolt and found it drawn. Someone had gone out ahead of me, and who would that be but Oskar? He had lied to me. He knew more than he'd revealed about the oberst, or else he was also suspicious of him or of Sigi, or he had, for who knows what reason, decided to leave without warning. I was getting out. I yanked the door, which opened with a grunt and a scrape, and stepped into the mist and damp. I took a leak on the lawn and started down the drive.

I was approaching the wall and the gate when I heard an accelerating rattle on the gravel behind me. I turned to see three big shepherd dogs, heads down, tongues out, racing toward me.

CHAPTER FIFTEEN

I don't like dogs. And dogs don't like me. Most of the time we avoid each other, but there was to be no nonaggression pact with these beasts. Leaping and slavering, they came out of the mist like Teutonic Hounds of the Baskervilles and, forgetting everything I knew about animals, I sprang for the gate. I got my hands on it, touched the substantial chain, and in sheer terror, leaped as high as I could to grasp the shafts of the spikes that decorated the top of the ironwork. The dogs were right behind me, barking and snarling now, as excited as hounds with a fox. I tried to swing my legs up high enough to get over the gate, but I was so stiff and short of breath with nerves that my first attempt failed.

A big breath. I swung my legs again, but before I could get my feet clear, one of the monstrous dogs grabbed my pant leg and set itself to pull me from the gate. It was a muscular, determined animal, and I saw a ghastly end and no final letter to poor Nan before I heard a faint whistle, so high as to be almost inaudible. It must have been a ghost whistle for monster dogs, because they stopped demanding my blood, although the one animal kept a death grip on my trousers. I turned my head cautiously, my arms beginning to tremble with the effort, and saw Oberst Weick walking unhurriedly down the drive. He was smoking the inevitable cigarette and carrying a pistol.

He said nothing until he was quite close to the gate, and then he spoke softly to the dogs. Instantly, the furry weight dropped from my leg, and the three brutes clustered around him, their big tails wagging, eager to receive some treat. Consolation, no doubt, for being denied filet of Francis. I came cautiously down the gate—one hand, then the other—and got my feet on the gravel. One pant leg was soaked from the dog's mouth, and, to collect myself, I rolled up the fabric and saw the bluish tooth marks but no blood.

"They are trained to hold, not to attack," the oberst said indifferently. He shifted his shoulder and bought his mechanical hand up for a puff of his cigarette.

The dogs sniffed around the grass and began pissing against the gate. Now that I was no longer of prime interest to them, I was angry. Dinner and a bed were all fine, but this was too high a price. "You set them on any guest who leaves early?"

"You might have been off with the silverware," he said calmly.

"I don't even have a knapsack." I turned out my pockets to show him that they were empty, too, although I really didn't think he was concerned about theft. "I went looking for the WC," I said. "I couldn't remember where it was, so I came outside."

"A long walk to take a leak," said the oberst.

I shrugged. "I was up. I was awake. I decided to head for the station."

He leaned over to the wall, stubbed out his cigarette, and knocked the butt from his mechanical fingers. "Enough," he said and gestured with his pistol for me to return to the house.

I shook my head. "Unlock the gate and I'll be gone. I don't think *der Bund* is really for me."

Oberst Weick raised the pistol. "It is so fortunate I was born left-handed," he said in a reflective tone. We might have been exchanging reminiscences over port in his study instead of standing in the mist with savage dogs. "They made me write with my right hand, but the war corrected that." He hefted the pistol as he spoke. "Now, please, let there be no misunderstanding. Should you be shot, it would be in the course of a robbery. A few well-placed pieces of silverware would do the trick absolutely."

I didn't like the sound of that at all. "It would be your word against mine," I said. "And there must be a British consulate in the area."

"There would be no word from you at all. I am an excellent shot, and with a Luger at this range, the outcome is not in doubt. Now you will come with me, Mr. Bacon."

My heart sank; this was worse than I'd thought, because my real name opened all sorts of dismal possibilities. Still, I made a show of resistance, swearing up and down that there was some mistake, that I knew nothing of this Bacon chap, that without a doubt my lost passport was at the bottom of everything.

The oberst said nothing, and I gradually fell silent. Then he said, "There are also the dogs. A word from me would be enough."

He didn't need to say more. This time when he gestured with the pistol, I started toward the house, a dog in front of me and one on either side. I followed the drive toward the front door, but the oberst directed me around the main building and past the stables to what looked to be a woodshed. "Open the door," he said.

A smell of logs, sawdust, decaying bark, and something else, too, made me hesitate to touch the latch, as all the bad feelings that had started with the sight of Oskar's empty bed flooded into my mind. Something hard, round, and metallic poked me in the left kidney. "Open the door."

I turned the knob and pushed the door. Something dark in the predawn light, something on the earthen floor. I stepped forward, frightened and sick. Someone was lying there on a dark stain. "Who?" I said. "Who?"

But before he could answer, I saw blond hair, and when I leaned down, I saw the perfect profile and one fine, pale hand. I heard a cry that exploded in the quiet dawn. And then another before the oberst hit me with the side of the pistol, and I realized it was my own voice. "Oskar! What has happened to Oskar! What have you done to him?"

"No, Mr. Bacon. It's what you've done to him. A lover's quarrel, maybe? Or something more sinister, connected with your uncle? The police can be here within minutes. I have only to call, but first we must talk."

He poked me again with the Luger and gestured toward the door. I stumbled out as if drunk, and, for I don't know how many minutes, all my senses were overwhelmed. Prodded by the oberst's gun, I must have passed the extensive vegetable gardens Oskar and I had admired only hours before, circled the stout turf-topped root cellar, and reached the edge of a grove of trees and a door. I was definitely standing before a door with brown paint set in a fieldstone building.

"Open it," said the oberst.

I hesitated. In a moment of near madness, I thought to myself, *He has only one arm—what if I grab his gun or can grab his good arm*, before one of the dogs nudged my leg with its large head. If I hurt the oberst in any way, they would kill me. I couldn't be sure of anything with Oberst Weick, but I felt that I could count on his dogs. I reached out, lifted the hasp that secured the door, and hauled it open. The Luger poked me in the back, and I stepped inside.

Stone floor, wood paneling, small windows protected by stout iron grills—a little cell, in short. There were two chairs and a wooden table, the whole smelling of mildew and permeated by a damp chill.

The oberst motioned for me to take one of the chairs and sat down himself. Panting noisily, the dogs explored the room before settling in the open doorway.

"You are in a bad position," he said.

"Put away the gun and send off the dogs and I'll be just fine." To my horror, I realized that my voice was trembling.

"I never understand English humor," he said. "I think every nation has its own laughter."

I was about to say that I didn't think Germans had any sense of humor but thought better of it. I shrugged. I was pretty sure the oberst didn't get up before dawn to discuss national styles in jokes. I might have followed that thought, but I could hear Nan saying, *Concentrate, Francis.* Not my best skill, especially when the main thing, the thing I must concentrate on, was the one thing I wanted not to see, not to hear, not to think about: Oskar lying dead.

"Oskar was a prince," I said.

The oberst blew out a column of smoke and watched it ascend toward the dark beams of the ceiling. "Even princes must be sacrificed sometimes. This is a cruel world."

"He was a patriot and an idealist!" I said. "What had he ever done but sell a few decks of snow in order to eat?"

"Oskar died for the Fatherland," the oberst said. "There is no more to be said about him. You, Mr. Bacon, are still very much alive. And perhaps would like to remain so."

I could have said, *You've killed Oskar, shoot me, too.* But I realized that I was not so romantic, that I was destined for an unglamorous survival. And then I thought that, given the opportunity, I could kill the oberst. That I would be capable of it. With this in mind, I asked what had happened.

"That's not for you to know. As far as the police are concerned, you and Oskar quarreled in the early hours and you stabbed him to death with a knife that you had removed from the dining room. Need I say that suggests forethought? The knife is there and will have your prints on it. Of course, your footprints are now in the woodshed. There may be other evidence needed, but be assured that we will supply whatever is required." He paused a moment and added, "I see you are stunned. Quite natural; you were never at the front." Once again his voice turned reflective. "At the front, such sights were a matter of course." He took another drag on his cigarette. "You can trust me when I say that if I summon the police, you will be the main suspect."

He paused to let this sink in. To be honest, I didn't absorb very much. I kept seeing the dark, distorted shape on the floor, and the horrible way that death had ruined Oskar.

"If I summon the police," the oberst repeated when I did not reply.

I looked up. I had not understood that any of this was conditional. "You must notify the police."

The oberst gave what without his scars would have passed for a smile. "I see that you are a law-abiding boy."

"Oskar is dead, murdered."

"But you are alive. And free. Perhaps even eager to return home? London has its attractions, I am sure."

I said nothing.

The oberst looked sharply at me and shook his head slightly. "Mr. Bacon, pull yourself together. We do not have much time." He turned his mechanical arm to look at his watch. "The sun will rise within the hour. The boys will get up. I will return from a walk with the dogs, and they will alert me to something in the woodshed. In the uproar, the police will be summoned and all will be set in motion."

I nodded. I could imagine that.

"Are you to be turned over to them, Mr. Bacon, as the likely suspect? Or are you to be safely hidden in this old gamekeeper's lodge? You must decide now."

This leap from suspect to safety was totally unexpected.

"What do you want from me? What is all this about? You know that I am completely innocent."

"What I know is flexible," the oberst said. "And you are not innocent at all. You are a plant from British intelligence and an associate of Lastings Marsdon, also known as Luc Pinot. Your uncle is a most dangerous man, Mr. Bacon."

In spite of my danger and distress, I almost laughed in his face. "You can't be serious. My uncle is a con man. He cheats suckers out of their money."

"He is a murderer," the oberst said. "And a spy. If he is cheating British intelligence, so much the better. But we still want him."

"A number of people want my uncle," I said.

"You have been in touch with him. We want to know where he is. Send a message telling him you need his help, and I will see that you escape the police."

"I have no idea where he is. He always contacted me, not the other way around. As far as I know, he's lined his pockets and is off looking for fresh pigeons."

The oberst took this under consideration. If he knew my real identity, I guessed that he knew a bit about Uncle Lastings. But not enough! The oberst was as bad as Harold and Mac and Miss F. How had they all been fooled? And why was I left to sort everything out?

"But," he said after a moment, "you are his nephew."

"He left me with an Adlon bill as big as the national debt, one guinea, six shillings, and fifteen marks. I haven't seen him since."

The Prussian mind likes precision, and I think the oberst was impressed by this exact accounting. "Yet you have survived," he said, and he raised the Luger.

My brain must have begun thawing, because in that gesture, I understood that innocence was more dangerous than guilt. The oberst was not interested in justice, and a genuine babe in the woods would be excess baggage for him. He'd murdered Oskar—and here I had the horrible thought that he'd murdered Oskar to force me to betray my uncle. He should have done it the other way around. I'd have betrayed Uncle Lastings to save Oskar any day.

But I'd been foolish to protest my innocence. If I had connections in high places and a line to my rascal of an uncle, I was valuable. If not, I was useless to the oberst, and what was to stop him from shooting me right here, right now? He hadn't spared Oskar, who was a patriot, a member of *der Bund*, and a model German citizen for the future. Worse, Oberst Weick had evidence of a sort, and I realized he could plausibly claim that, handicapped as he was, he had no choice but to shoot me. And if he did, I certainly believed that the outcome would not be in doubt.

I was clearly safer guilty. "Uncle Lastings is out of reach," I said, "but he had some friends. More pigeons. Perhaps a message to one of them?"

The oberst thought this over, while I wondered who best to mention. Please remember, I didn't ask for any of this.

"He does send messages—at least he did before his contact was murdered," I continued, "but I never read them." I assumed that the oberst already knew all about Belinda. Most likely he'd had her killed.

"And who does read them?" he asked, raising his weapon slightly.

"Mac. He's called Mac."

"In all of Berlin," the oberst said sarcastically, "one man called Mac."

"He's attached to the embassy."

"Not good enough," said the oberst. "A phony diplomat attached to the embassy. They are a dime a dozen. Every embassy has them. You must do better."

I hesitated until he grew impatient. "There are always the dogs. I find men are most afraid of either guns or dogs. I can see you lean toward the latter."

"I deal with Mac—and my landlady."

"Really?"

"Clarice Fallowfield."

"Ah, English. I might have known." The oberst glanced down at the Luger with what might have been regret. "I will bring paper," he said and stood up.

"Where am I to be hidden?" I asked. "The police will surely search all the outbuildings."

The oberst raised his head and gave me a haughty look. "They will have my word that this building—like many others—was locked. The main gate will be open. It will appear that you made for the station and the rail line."

With this, he rose and, followed by the dogs, went outside. I heard the metallic rattle as he locked the door. From one of the small windows I watched his progress across the field toward the gardens and the house. Now that he wasn't prodding me with the pistol, he had managed to set up another cigarette. I could see the smoke rising. I couldn't quite imagine the mind that could shoot an acquaintance before dawn, threaten another before breakfast, and stroll back to call the police as if this was an ordinary morning.

I was in big trouble. At some point, the oberst would return. Immediately, if he should delay summoning the police. Otherwise, I guessed there would be a fair amount of time devoted to helping with inquiries, as the phrase goes, and playing lord of the manor to forestall a serious search. All the boys would be questioned. That would take time. And the staff, too. If the gate was open, that raised other possibilities. Oh, yes, the police would be busy. Meanwhile, I stood shivering all over, more from nerves than cold, trying to decide whom to contact. I was sorry to have mentioned Miss Fallowfield, although I suspected that she could take care of herself.

Naming Harold would have been poetic justice, but he was too high up in the embassy. They might not believe me or—worse—he might not be inclined to help. That left Mac. So far as I could trust any of them, I thought a note to Mac was my best bet. And what to say? *Am being held hostage by fanatical German nationalists? Send the head of Uncle Lastings?*

That's what they wanted, but the appeal lacked something, and I didn't think it would be effective. *Fanatics willing to swap me for Lastings. Remember I'm only seventeen.* How's that? An appeal to Mac's better nature and sentimental side, if he has one? Very good, but I was pretty sure that Uncle L. had done a bunk. Could he be summoned out of thin air, even the rarified air of cafés and clubs like the Eldorado? And even if by some chance my uncle had found a courier despite his shortage of funds, and if Mac went to the Eldorado and made contact and sent on my cry for help, would Uncle Lastings drop whatever he was enjoying to put his head on the block? I knew my uncle too well to imagine that!

The best thing I could do would be to play along with the oberst and hope to escape. That seemed such a tall order that I wondered whether I might be better off with the police. But that would involve questioning, and not just about Oskar, who I kept seeing sprawled in the half-light of the shed. The police would want to know about delivering the Webley to my uncle and careening around the dark streets afterward to the station. I might eventually be found innocent of Oskar's murder, but I'd clearly be guilty of something.

I stamped around the little lodge and banged my fist on the table, and very nearly dismembered a chair, before I calmed down. Possibly there was a way out. If so, I needed to find it. And if not, I needed to look for some weapon, because even if I wrote the note he wanted, and even if by some miracle Uncle Lastings replied, I doubted very much that my safe exit was on Oberst Weick's program.

CHAPTER SIXTEEN

I surveyed my cell and considered my options. The chairs were sturdy, as was the table. Could I take apart one or the other? Possible, but I didn't think even a stout piece of oak was going to thwart a man with a Luger, not to mention dogs. There was a sink in one corner, equipped with a hand pump. I worked the handle for a minute. Although a bit rusty, the water was drinkable. I was not to die of thirst.

Could the handle be removed? I fiddled with it for a bit, but the pump was well constructed and the handle solidly fastened. I took a turn around the room and checked the bars on the windows. Why did a gamekeeper's lodge have barred windows to start with? A question, I suspected, with no pleasant answer. Rafters up top, broad enough to hold me, I was sure. Though I might be able to climb up and escape the dogs, I would be a sitting target for the oberst.

Floor next. Some storage hatch? A trap door entrance to some basement space? No chance. The oberst had picked his spot carefully. I am not fond of confined spaces, and bullying types like him provoke bad memories. I started shivering again, and I thought it would be nice if there was a fire in the fireplace. It was certainly a big, impressive one with old-fashioned fittings. Someone had cooked in this years ago and probably smoked pork or game more recently.

I stepped closer and craned my neck. The flue was black with soot but surprisingly wide. Wide enough for a sweep? One of those sad little Victorian boys in the stories Nan used to read me? I thought so. Wide enough for an adult? A bit less certain. I went to the windows again, checked the grills, looked out toward the gardens, the stables, and the main house.

I should hear the carriage returning with officers, maybe even a police motorcycle brought over on the ferry. At the very least, there should be voices near the woodshed, the directions and observations of the functionaries of violent death. Surely the boys would be out gawking and noisy with questions. There would be shouts and instructions and complaints. Yet I heard nothing but the soft sound of pigeons in the wood and far off, the sound of someone working with an ax.

Had the oberst delayed contacting the police for some reason? I worried about this question for a minute, and then I remembered something else: the discussion Mac, Harold, and Miss F. had early on about an informant in the embassy. Someone there had passed on information about my meeting with Harold at the Romanisches Café. If they were right, and if the oberst knew that person, he hadn't needed any message from me. All he'd needed was to discover my contacts.

Which meant I was already irrelevant. Oberst Weick had gotten what he wanted, and the only good thing about the transaction was that I had neither been shot nor bitten—yet. He would return, though, and what was to prevent him from killing me? He'd been tempted earlier; perhaps he was only waiting to see if I had lied to him. Perhaps he was even now set to contact not the police, but his associates in Berlin. I suspected that one of them would go after Miss Fallowfield. She needed to be warned, and I needed to get out.

I checked the windows one last time and stepped into the big fireplace. I put one foot on a firedog, the other on one of the sturdy pot racks and pushed my hands flat against the greasy, soot-covered walls of the chimney. I really should have paid more attention to my physical culture classes. Even a little of Sigi's *Wehrsport* would be useful. I braced one knee against the slick wall of the flue and got my other leg a few inches higher. *Press with both hands, move up a few inches. Slide hands up but don't slip back. Brace and inch higher. This isn't going to work*, I thought, then I heard a rattle at the door and decided that it had to.

A creak escaped as the door opened. Was my trailing foot visible? *Don't breathe, don't move.* Easier said than done when my arms were beginning to tremble from the strain. *Push against the sides, keep still.* There were footsteps below as the oberst circled the room. Despite all that Prussian restraint, he had a fine line in barracks profanity. *The dogs will give me away*, I thought, *and he'll shoot for sure.* But no rattle of nails, no slobbering panting, no dogs. Of course, I realized, he doesn't need them if he is going to kill me right here, right now.

Should I drop down and try for surprise? I closed my eyes. *Don't breathe, don't gasp*, I told myself, as the smells of old grease and soot, rising up my nose and tickling the back of my throat, crept inevitably toward my lungs. Any minute, any second, I'd start to wheeze. I took a quick little breath that was nonetheless loud in my ears. *He'll come now. There will be a shot. Good-bye, Nan.* I might have been heroic after all and refused to tell the oberst anything or told him to shoot me back in the woodshed. It was going to amount to the same thing in the end.

Which was now: *Bang!* I was so startled I almost fell onto the hearth. But no pain. An instant transformation into the afterlife? I remind myself that I do not believe in an after. Besides, I was still squeezed between the filthy sides of a soot-encrusted chimney. I looked down. Blood dripping from my legs? No. Pain? Just aching muscles everywhere. Footsteps of the prowling oberst with homicide on his mind? None whatsoever.

I realized that he hadn't seen me, that he thought I'd vanished into thin air like my larcenous uncle. I enjoyed a moment of triumph before I remembered the dogs. He was going back for them. Arms trembling, I let myself slide down the chimney, stumbled onto the hearth and, bent double to avoid the windows, reached the door. I gave it a successful push. With the horse gone, so to speak, he hadn't bothered to lock up.

You can bet I legged it out of there. I was into the woods and onto a gravel road before I realized this would not do at all. I didn't know the terrain, and without a bike, I'd never keep ahead of the dogs. I stood on the road for several minutes thinking of this plan and that, and rejecting all of them, before I understood what I had to do: I had to return to the gamekeeper's lodge and hide there until the dogs were well past.

I started running before I could think how much I disliked the idea and how hard it was going to be to open the lodge door and wait inside for the oberst to pass by with those big slavering brutes that would bark and jump and beg to be let into the lodge. That didn't bear thinking about. In spite of my resolve, I gradually slowed my pace. I reached the lodge and forced myself inside just moments before I heard the dogs.

I lay down on the floor first but, feeling too exposed, I jumped up to stand pressed against the wall at the side of the door. Should the oberst think to peek in, he might not see me. Then I waited, my heart hammering with nerves and exertion. A shrill bark before, horror of horrors, the scrape and rattle of doggy nails against the door. The oberst shouted angrily, and after a few seconds, the dogs subsided. I'd guessed right: He was not a man to take direction from animals.

I moved cautiously to the rear window. They were heading into the woods, the dogs with their noses down and their tails wagging, all excited at the prospect of running me down. When they were out of sight, I opened the door and moved as quickly as I could without actually running. My thought was to circle the outbuildings to the shrubs and trees near the main house. When the coast was clear, I'd leave on the road to Stralsund. Or, if there were police about, I'd head back to Putbus and sleep on the beach.

How foolish I'd been not to tell Miss Fallowfield that I was going to the island. And how shortsighted to imagine that the area would have telephone service. I was stranded, virtually without money, and pursued by killer dogs. With these miseries in mind, I was close to the house before I realized how quiet every-thing was. Where was *der Bund*? Where were the police? Was it possible that they had still not arrived?

I was guessing that it was ten, maybe even eleven, o'clock. I'd seen the oberst's carriage parked on the drive, and he had a stable full of horses to pull it. Even quicker, he could have sent a groom on horseback. Fifteen or twenty minutes to the ferry, which made regular crossings. As long again to get to Stralsund and find a telephone, possibly right at the ferry office. As for the police, they would surely have a boat of their own. They should already be here, unless the oberst had wanted to get the members of *der Bund* out of the way first.

I tried to make myself approach the house casually, not easy to do when I was black with grease and soot and half-paralyzed with nerves. Sounds of voices and rattling pots issued from the kitchen. I avoided that window and slipped along the side of the house. Fortunately, the oberst favored yews and other conifers close to the building. I moved carefully to the front and checked the drive for bicycles.

Only two machines remained. *Der Bund* was clearly gone. I was wondering how the oberst had explained our absence, when I heard footsteps on the porch. A man came down onto the drive and, to my alarm, turned in my direction. *Back into the bushes, Francis!*

I retreated as fast as I could without snapping a branch or tripping on a root. I squeezed behind one of the large yews and froze, for the fellow now stopped his stroll and lit a ciga-rette almost directly in front of me. He tipped his head back to watch the smoke ascend. A contemplative sort, clearly, with his mind on—what? That was the question. Higher things? Was this just a casual visitor, or was he a partner in crime with the oberst? I stood so still and tensely that I started getting cramps in my legs. Worse yet, I saw that what I had assumed was a riding crop or an old swagger stick tucked under his arm was actually a golf putter. I'd thought that a strictly Anglo-Saxon vice. And maybe it was because on closer examination there was something not quite "Prussian officer" about this one.

Our mystery visitor finished his cigarette and flipped the butt into the shrubbery. Then he took a golf ball from his pocket, tossed it onto the grass, and began lining up putts. I hoped that this might lead him away from the house, but no. He putted in one direction then turned and worked his way back, softly whistling a jaunty march that seemed vaguely familiar. Perhaps I'd have identified the tune if I hadn't been so alarmed about my prospects, for it began to look as if I would be trapped in the shrubbery until the oberst returned with his dogs. And wouldn't they be excited when they sniffed me out.

I felt for the wall behind me, thinking to make my way around the house in the other direction, and touched a windowsill. The sash was open. Some tidy housemaid had aired the dining room after the smoke of the night before. Without giving it another thought, I climbed in. I was headed for the front door, when I heard the crunch of horses' hooves on the gravel outside. I pivoted to the main staircase and reached the top as the oberst's butler emerged to open the front door.

Up another flight, Francis. Would they have already swept the attic room? I put my money and a good deal more on Prussian efficiency and eased open the door to the dormitory I'd left only hours before. I was ready with a story about a dropped scarf, a quick return from the run to the ferry, various ingenious and charming lies, but the room was clean, shipshape, and empty. I suddenly felt exhausted. I lay down on one of the cots and fell asleep.

•   •   •

When I woke up, the light was low; I'd slept half the day away. My head was throbbing, my mouth was dry, and I was desperately thirsty. But what woke me was a presence in the room, someone moving cautiously between the cots. Not a chambermaid. And not the oberst, either. The figure bumped into a cot, recovered, then swayed toward the low arched windows that brought in the only light.

I lay perfectly still and watched him—yes, it was definitely male—out of the corner of my eye. I found something familiar about his silhouette, but not his gait. Then I sat up with a jerk as a ghost, a specter, the sum of childhood fears came to life. Nan was wrong: Phantoms did exist and this one lunged across the space between the cots and grabbed for me before slumping onto the floor.

"Don't shout!" Oskar said. "Please, it's me." His face was pale and his wonderful eyes very dark.

"You were stabbed. I saw you lying in a pool of blood in the woodshed."

He shook his head.

"Oberst Weick said that you were stabbed to death. He threatened to tell the police I had killed you." I could hear my voice going up a register, but already my perspective was changing. The hand on my knee was warm if very dirty, and though I could see dried blood on Oskar's face, he seemed to belong very much in the here and now. "What happened to you?"

He shook his head. "Where is everyone?"

"*Der Bund* is gone. The bikes are gone. You've been missing all day."

Oskar pulled himself up and sat next to me on the cot. There was blood on his face and the hair on the top of his head was dark and matted.

"You were struck on the head," I suggested.

He put his hand up. "I saw," he began and stopped. "I got up in the night," he said after a long silence. "I went down to the toilet. I heard voices below and looked over the rail."

He made another helpless gesture. "Something happened, but I can't remember."

"The boys were all asleep."

"Not one of us, no."

"The household staff too, probably."

"He sounded like you," Oskar said after a minute. "Not the voice but the accent."

"Tall and thin? Military probably?"

"I think," Oskar said. "But I can't really remember."

"I saw him but he did not see me." Fortunately! "We must get away from here," I said. "We are not safe."

"I don't know how far I can walk." Oskar lifted his pant leg to show me a big raw wound on his calf. "I was maybe shot?"

Maybe. The wound was still oozing blood, and I did not like to think of how dirty it might be after the woodshed. I took off my shirt and, after a struggle, tore off both sleeves. "The wounds need to be washed," I said.

There was a sink with a cold tap in the corridor between the dormitory and the staff quarters. I went out cautiously, but the household must have been busy with dinner preparations, for there was no one about. I took a big drink, then soaked one of the sleeves and washed Oskar's wounded leg and got most of the blood out of his hair and off his face.

He'd had some first-aid training and showed me how to bandage his wound with the other sleeve. Then we sat shivering and half-dizzy with hunger and tried to think what to do next.

"Does he let the dogs out at night?"

Oskar thought about this. His mental processes had slowed to a crawl. "I don't think so."

"He had them out for a walk very early in the morning."

"I think that is right."

"We'll wait until dark and leave once everyone is asleep. There are two bikes left."

"The gate will be locked," Oskar said. "That I know. And I am not sure I could pedal a bike."

I told him about the gravel track I'd discovered beyond the woods. "There is no wall there. It probably curves around to the main road."

Oskar agreed this would be our best bet; he certainly had

no other suggestion. He lay down on one of the cots, groaning occasionally from the pain in his leg. After a bit, he fell asleep, leaving me to wonder about his injuries and to fight the temptation to try for some food. I kept watch at the windows, too, and just at dusk, I heard the rattle of wheels and the hollow clomp of hooves. I looked out. A trap pulled by a handsome black pony was waiting at the front door. Out came the tall, thin man I'd seen from the shrubbery, accompanied by the oberst and the inevitable dogs. A few words, then the visitor got into the passenger's seat. The groom hopped in beside him and took up the reins.

Off they went. Surely to Stralsund, probably to Berlin, possibly to Miss Fallowfield's. I fussed about when we could most safely leave and tried not to think about dinner while Oskar slept on. Once it was dark, I eased the door a crack to listen for the weary staff mounting the stairs and for the sound of water emptying from the cistern in the oberst's WC. Lucky man. I made do with a piss out the window.

Finally, the big house seemed quiet. I went over to the cot where Oskar was lying. He'd lost blood, but it was his head that worried me more. What if he didn't wake up or woke up completely disoriented? "Oskar," I whispered before I could put myself into a panic. "Oskar."

"What time is it?"

"I don't know. You have a watch."

He raised his arm and held the watch to his ear then wound it. "Nearly midnight."

"Do you think the oberst will be asleep?"

Oskar shrugged.

"His visitor has gone."

"Then possibly."

"Do you know where the dogs will be?"

"In a room off the kitchen. They're closed up for the night. I remember that," Oskar said with more animation than he had shown so far. "No dogs."

I wondered if they would remember my smell. If a whiff of Francis would interrupt their dreams. If they would rouse the house. I was trouble, but Oskar might be worse. I'd been threatened but unharmed. Oskar had been injured badly enough for him to forget what had happened to him. But the oberst would not know that.

CHAPTER SEVENTEEN

I got Oskar onto his feet. He seemed even less steady than before, and when his arm was draped over my shoulders, he felt hot. Out in the corridor, I got him to drink some water, then we started down the stairs—a nerve-racking business, because he could not put full weight on his injured leg. Even with the carpeting on the stairs, our progress seemed noisy to me, and on every step, I had visions of the oberst emerging in his nightshirt with Luger in hand.

Across the corridor to the main stairs, Oskar swayed with each step. A run on bikes was unimaginable, but he was too sick to abandon to the attic. *Get out first*, I told myself, *plan later*. Onto the main stairs. Oskar kept a death grip on the oak railing and edged down with my help to the first landing. The stone floor looked very far below, and Oskar suddenly tensed up. "Keep going," I whispered.

"I fell here."

That might explain the wound on his head. But still, the oberst with all his military experience must have known that

Oskar was alive. Must have. And must be still looking for him. "Oskar, we need to get out of here."

Down to the foyer. "Catch your breath," I said, leaving him propped against a chest. I crept into the adjoining dining room and felt along the table. Not even a crumb. Over to the sideboard. Surely, they would be set up for breakfast. I touched a dish, rattling its metal cover, froze, then spotted a round loaf of bread. I tucked it under my sweater and returned to Oskar, who stood drooping with his head down, only half-conscious.

To the door. Slide the bolt. *Was that a whine from one of the dogs? Don't think about that. Thinking about it will make it happen. Think sleeping dogs. Dreaming dogs.* I pushed the door open and pulled Oskar outside, where the moonlight and clouds cast our enormous shadows. We left the noisy gravel for a grassy path toward the outbuildings and the woods, but we had barely reached the first paddock when Oskar stopped.

"You go on, Francis," he said clutching the fence. "Get help. I'll hide somewhere here."

He was shaking with fever, and I feared it was all over. It was several miles to the ferry dock, and clearly Oskar would never manage the distance on foot. But the spring night was cold, and in the stable, the warmest place for him, the first groom up in the morning would discover him. Even if I found help—and this was an ungodly hour by Rügen standards—no one around here would care to tackle the oberst: *I understand, Herr Oberst, that you have shot a guest?* Not a very likely conversation.

"It's too cold for you. You're feverish, and you need that wound cleaned." I thought the stable would surely have iodine, and, with the fatal smell of horse already tickling my nose, I dragged him into the tack room, hoping that the grooms, if they slept in the stable, were safely up in the loft. In the dim light, I found bottles lined up on a shelf. Liniment from the smell of the first couple. Whiskey in another. I stuck that in my pocket. Iodine in the next? I thought so. I put that bottle in Oskar's jacket for the moment. Horse iodine was strong; it would burn like hell and maybe he'd scream. Not here!

I found a bridle and lifted one of the saddles from its rack, took a deep breath, and went into the corridor between the stalls to look for a strong, placid horse. Such as my father used to put me up on, placid being his only concession to the fact that horseflesh swelled my eyes and closed up my lungs. *Poor Francis has asthma*, Nan would say. *Nonsense! The boy's a born malingerer.* That was Pater, of course, who, like the oberst, didn't take suggestions easily. *It's all in his head.*

Much as I hated to agree in any way with my father, tonight I had to pretend that he was right. I knew how to tack up a horse, and I knew how to ride. I was going to put Oskar on the back of what looked to be a fine Hanoverian. I was going to take him to the ferry dock, where I would dump what I hoped was horse iodine on his leg and get him to safety. That was the plan, and though I sneezed uncontrollably once, I got the horse ready, tied it at the door of the stable, and maneuvered Oskar to the mounting block.

After a fine struggle and a momentary faint from Oskar, I got him onto the horse. I climbed into the saddle, and with his arms locked around my waist, I took up the reins and clucked to the horse. It threw its head up and down in irritation before setting off into the woods and onto the gravel road. My eyes were already itching, but I knew better than to rub them. Fortunately, I had picked wisely. The horse seemed to know the way and, although my eyes were soon watering so that I could hardly see, we moved smartly along the track until we joined the road to the Stralsund ferry. "We're going to manage this," I told Oskar.

He groaned in reply, his head slumped against my shoulder, and by the time we saw the glitter of the Baltic and the silhouette of the ferry port and the keeper's house, anxiety about Oskar had almost replaced my fear of discovery. At the ferry dock, I pulled up the horse, slid down, and lifted a semiconscious Oskar from the saddle. The horse ambled to the verge and began to crop the grass by the side of the road, while I half-carried and half-dragged my friend to the ferry keeper's house. I pounded at the door. *Helfen Sie mir! Helfen Sie mir!*

At last, a man with his trousers pulled up over a nightshirt appeared. In the light of his oil lamp, I saw a bony face, a broken nose, and hair and eyebrows so light as to appear white, although he seemed quite young. My friend has been badly injured, I told him, shot, an accident with a gun. Fever, infection—I threw in everything but the oberst and the pursuit of killer dogs. I must have seemed convincing despite, or maybe because of, my filthy appearance and streaming eyes. He set down the lamp and helped me carry Oskar into the house, where we laid him on a battered couch. I held up the bottles I'd filched to the light. One was indeed iodine. The other was whiskey. I gave the ferryman the first drink and took one myself.

Believe me, on my empty stomach it went right to work. Thus fortified, I rolled up Oskar's trouser leg to reveal the bandage, already a mess of blood and not nearly as clean as I'd hoped. The ferryman held up his hand and told me to wait. He got a pot, pumped some water, then lit his stove. He found a knife, and once the water had warmed up, we soaked and cut the bandage from the wound.

"Bad," he said. "This needs a doctor."

"Is there anyone on the island?" I regretted that I'd released the horse. I could perhaps have gone for assistance.

He shook his head. "I can take you across to the hospital at first light."

I thought that with luck, the oberst and his monster dogs would not be out before dawn.

We cleaned up Oskar's head, the ferryman cutting away some matted hair, and dumped iodine on both wounds, producing a shriek loud enough to wake half the island. After this treatment, Oskar deserved the last of the whiskey, and I produced the loaf, rather the worse for our adventures, and cut off a piece for each of us. Oskar managed a few mouthfuls before he passed out again.

I went through his wallet. Between us, we had enough for the ferryman, and as soon as the sky began to lighten, he was as good as his word. Either he was an early riser or my ill-concealed nervousness had transmitted itself to him. Probably both, for the ferryman would surely know Oberst Weick and the boys of *der Bund*. He might even have recognized the horse, and nothing good was going to come of the midnight arrival of a wounded man on one of the oberst's animals.

We carried Oskar to the boat wrapped in an old blanket. The ferryman started the engine, and we sailed into a dank sea breeze that cleared my lungs of hay and horses. On the Stralsund dock, the island ferryman had an extended confab with his onshore counterpart. The upshot was that we parted with our last marks and were put into the hands of a local carter. He was due to deliver supplies to the island, but he put Oskar on top of the load and, with me on the seat beside him, made a detour to the hospital.

I worried that, broke as we were, Oskar wouldn't be admitted, but when I said that his father was a professor, the carter snorted. "Insurance for him, not to worry. All workers and dependents."

That was a huge relief. I made up a cock-and-bull story for the admitting resident and saw Oskar safely stowed in a ward. I took advantage of a hospital washroom to improve my appearance and to turn my filthy sweater inside out. Next step on the program: telegrams and breakfast, because I was feeling lightheaded. Fortunately, the area near the ferry and the hospital was full of carters and porters and gents with business on their minds, one of whom caught my eye. He was stout, prosperous, and middle-aged with graying hair and bright black eyes that I found attractive. We easily came to an agreement. Thanks to Uncle Lastings, I'd learned a thing or two in Berlin.

But first, a detour to the telegraph office, where I composed a message to Oskar's father. Short, quick, and cheap: *Oskar injured Stop In Stralsund Hospital Stop.* And one a little more difficult to Miss Fallowfield: *Thin ex-military who whistles possible mole Stop Visited Oberst Weick on Rügen Stop Weick knows you Mac Stop*

Will return Berlin Stop. I handed over the coins and winked at my gent, who was quite satisfactory and treated me to a bang-up breakfast of wurst, sausage, bread, cheese, and a big stein of beer later at the station.

When I had my return ticket in my pocket, everything seemed so in order that I decided to take a later train to Berlin, even if it was a local, to see how Oskar was doing. He was *resting comfortably* said the attending doctor, small and Jewish with very white hands and a melancholy expression on his long, thin face. He nodded his approval when I said I'd sent a telegram to Oskar's father.

"Very good. If the wound stays clean, he will recover nicely."

I didn't like that *if.* "And if not?"

He looked down and touched the stethoscope hanging around his neck. "Your friend could be very ill—or lose his leg."

I was horrified, especially because I felt that I had somehow caused Oskar's injury.

The doctor patted my shoulder gently. "We can have hope," he said. "The iodine must have been very strong because it burned the wound. Still, the best thing you could have done under the circumstances. And his father is coming. That is good, too. Now, I must see to my rounds." He gestured for me to enter the ward, a big drafty room with a high ceiling and tall windows that brought in the cool Baltic light. Only a couple of beds were occupied, and there was a chair free, which I pulled over next to Oskar's bed.

His head was wrapped in a white turban, and they had a rack of some sort under the covers to keep the weight of the sheets off his injured leg. Despite his beautiful tan, he was pale, and his face seemed to have grown thinner and sharper in the night. One of his hands was lying outside the blanket. I put my hand on it, then touched his forehead. He did not seem quite so hot. Perhaps he would be all right. He had to be.

I sat there for what seemed like a long time, and I was beginning to think I must get to the station, when Oskar opened his eyes. "Francis." He mumbled something in German that I could not catch.

"You're in the hospital," I said. "The doctor says you are doing fine."

He was silent for a moment. When he spoke, it was again in German; apparently, English was now too difficult for him to manage. "I was shot."

"Yes. Do you know who shot you?"

I thought he would say the oberst, but I was wrong. "Underwood. His name is Underwood. He is English, I think. Maybe Irish."

That was an unwelcome surprise. I thought I had understood what was up, but apparently not. "Why, Oskar?"

"Because I recognized him. I need to tell you something, Francis, then you must leave and stay away."

"I'm on the next train to Berlin."

He struggled to sit up, but the effort made him clutch his head in pain. I helped him lie back down.

"Rest and don't worry," I said.

He seized my hand in agitation. "Don't go to the Eldorado. Don't go near it."

"Why not, Oskar?"

"We were watching the club."

"*Der Bund*, you mean?"

He moved his head a fraction and winced. "Underwood paid me. To tell him who were the regulars. Especially British or foreign regulars. I think he killed your friend." He pressed my hand. "I am so sorry, Francis. I did not know what they had in mind. They threatened to have me arrested for dealing snow. And because the oberst has some in with the police, I think he could have made it happen. That would have about killed my father."

"I sent him a telegram. He had to know you're in the hospital."

Oskar closed his eyes for a moment as if deeply pained. I was not sure I would have wanted my father summoned if our positions had been reversed, but a respectable father would be about the best protection Oskar could have.

"You'll be all right," I said and rose to go, but he gripped my hand.

"Underwood was there the night of the murder. I saw him talking with the big drag queen. Then a couple customers came up, and by the time they were gone, so were Underwood and your friend. I told myself it was coincidence."

I could believe that. I'd probably have told myself the same thing. "But why would he shoot you now? The investigation hasn't produced anything."

"I think it was because of you, Francis. I was told to bring you to Rügen. I thought it would be like with me, that they would pay you to watch people at the Eldorado. But I think now it was because of your uncle. Oberst Weick and Underwood were arguing about something when they saw me. Underwood was startled." Oskar raised his hand like a gun. "Long. There was something long on the pistol. I heard a small noise and"—he moved his hand—"then nothing. I must have fallen down the stairs, but I don't remember anything until I was back in the attic and I saw you sit up on the cot."

"Yet you were not killed."

"No. The oberst would have been against it. Your friend was foreign, a Pole, possibly a Jew. The police would not exert themselves. I would be a different case. I think the oberst explained that to Underwood."

Oskar sank back on the pillows, and this time when he closed his eyes, I saw that he had fallen asleep. I sat for a few moments, anyway. Underwood had been nervous enough to shoot Oskar more or less on sight. Yet just hours later, he was out practicing his putting as if he hadn't a care in the world. Had the oberst convinced him that Oskar was dying or dead? Or had Underwood planned to dispatch my friend—and maybe me, too—later and farther away from the oberst's estate? If so, what Nan would have called our *midnight flit* had disrupted that plan.

Hopefully permanently, I thought. I stroked Oskar's forehead and stood up with real regret. I liked him, although I now suspected that all along I had been less a romantic interest than a target. I might have been angry about that if poor Oskar hadn't paid so dearly for the deception. A head injury, possibly a damaged, even a lost, leg. And all because of a martinet like the oberst and a weasel like Underwood, not to mention a whole lot of patriotic hot air. *Save me from drums and uniforms*, I thought, and with one more regretful glance—even now he was still a prince—I left the ward.

CHAPTER EIGHTEEN

I got a cup of coffee at the station buffet to be sure I would be awake when the Berlin train arrived. I wanted to get away from Stralsund as soon as possible, even though I felt guilty about leaving Oskar, and frightened for him, too, because the hospital had people coming and going at all hours. My best hope was that his father would arrive soon, full of Prussian efficiency and Berlin attitude. I could imagine that reunion all too well, and my presence would not be required. At least, that's how I rationalized my run to Berlin, where His Majesty's Secret Whatever would surely spirit me away from Prussian reformatories and political fanatics.

I went out onto the platform the minute the intercity was announced. I was watching the disembarking passengers and looking for the third-class carriages and generally feeling bad and nervous and impatient, when someone touched my shoulder.

"Francis! Francis Wood, I believe."

I turned and almost jumped out of my skin. Underwood stood there, tall, thin, and one hundred percent ex-military. An attaché case instead of a putter this time. He wasn't whistling, either, but there was no doubt that this was the gent who'd practiced his golf on the oberst's lawn and who'd shot Oskar the night before. I would have given myself away if I hadn't been momentarily rendered speechless.

I pulled away from him. "I don't believe I've had the pleasure," I said.

"My apologies!" He was suddenly all flutter and charm, a classic twit act hiding something lethal. "I've been following your career with such interest. Of course, I've processed your documents and photos." He stuck his hand out. "Aubrey Underwood, British embassy. At your service."

I doubted that very much, but there was nothing to do but shake his hand. "You are here on a holiday?"

He laughed, a big false laugh showing the worst of British dentistry. "No, no. I'm here for you. There was anxiety at the embassy. Now, we must talk." He put his hand on my shoulder and attempted to steer me toward the station buffet.

Even if my telegram to Miss Fallowfield had been delivered instantly, and even if she had somehow misunderstood my message, there would not have been time for the treacherous Underwood to have caught the Berlin train and made the three- or four-hour journey to Stralsund. "Really? How did the embassy know where I was?" I tried to sound like an only mildly paranoid citizen.

"Trade craft, Francis. I can call you Francis, can't I?"

I didn't respond.

"There was concern, you can be sure, when you went missing. Perhaps, we thought, he is off on a *Bummel*—wonderful Deutsch word, don't you agree? Or with *der Wandervogel?* I wouldn't have thought the outdoor life your style, but perhaps there were compensations." Here he gave me a keen look.

"So I cut work. I don't think the Eldorado called the embassy." As I spoke, I edged back toward the platform.

"Your inestimable landlady contacted us."

I was startled by this and wondered if I had calculated the train times incorrectly; Nan always said that my mental arithmetic needed improvement. Worse, maybe Miss F. and Mac and Harold—Harold, whom I disliked and had never trusted—had decided that I was more trouble than I was worth.

Fortunately, Underwood was too busy playing up his all-so-innocent concern to register my alarm. "The blotter, don't you know, tells the tale. And your habit of writing to your old nanny! It does you credit, Francis, but it leaves a record."

I understood then. My description of a jolly trip to the island had left a reverse imprint on the blotter—just the sort of thing Miss F. would spot. But that meant she had alerted the embassy before my telegram. I hadn't been betrayed after all, and I just had to keep my head.

"This train returns to Berlin in a few minutes. I need to be on it. My job's kaput if I'm not at work tonight."

"We need to talk," he repeated and took hold of my arm.

I planted my feet and shook my head. "Talk to me on the train."

"You're not the only one involved," he said, and added in an undertone, "Oskar Schafer. He is of interest to the embassy. We have been keeping an eye on him, but he did not return with the rest of *der Bund*. Where is he?"

I jerked my arm away, and if I'd had a weapon I'd have injured him. "Oskar is dead. Murdered." I let my voice rise, causing a couple travelers to turn and look.

Underwood bit his lip, which told me that he did not want a scene. Could I rely on that to get him onto the train—and keep Oskar temporarily safe? It was worth a try. In my loudest, coarsest German I denounced him as a sugar licker and suggested a number of interesting things he might do to himself.

Underwood flushed scarlet and, seizing my arm again, propelled me toward the train. I protested but not so vigorously that we were prevented from entering a first-class carriage. He pushed me into an empty compartment.

"That little scene was quite uncalled for," he said, putting his attaché case at his feet. I could see that he was torn between the desire to maintain his pose as my concerned friend and a strong impulse to thump me a good one.

"Was it? You want to keep me in Stralsund when my friend is dead. I'm not safe here."

"Of course, of course. That is quite, quite understandable."

I wondered if he always repeated himself when he was lying. *Don't be too clever, Francis*, Nan said in my ear. This was a man who had shot Oskar with a silencer and probably killed Belinda the same way. He would undoubtedly have other skills. Our compartment was otherwise empty, the whole carriage only half-full, and as the train pulled from the station, I wondered if I had miscalculated. I didn't fancy being alone in a compartment with him.

But Underwood, who seemed alternately rigid and slippery, now set himself to be solicitous. "Oskar Schafer dead! Such a young fellow! Now you said 'murdered.' But you were, of course, exaggerating. Natural under the emotion of the moment."

I waited to see where he was going with this.

"Could Oskar's death have been an accident? Isn't that possible?"

I shrugged. "Oskar is dead is all I know."

"It had to have been an accident," Underwood said in such a reasonable tone that, if I hadn't seen him on the oberst's lawn and known what had happened, I would have believed every word. "Because who would have wanted to hurt him?"

"We were all his friends," I admitted. Inspired, I added, "Though Sigi was jealous of him."

"Who is this Sigi?"

I said that he worked at the Eldorado as a dancer.

Underwood lit a cigarette and watched the smoke for a moment as if this was all news to him. "Possible, I suppose," he said. I had to wait for whatever else he had in mind, because the conductor arrived and tickets had to be purchased. Underwood's German was rapid and precise. He was chatty with the conductor, mentioning that he had been sent to collect a young relative with certain problems. The Kripos had been involved. Outbursts such as the one on the platform were not unusual. Drugs were likely a factor.

I kept my face noncommittal, although I could see that Underwood was covering his backside in case of any future unpleasantness. I had made a mistake with that hint of a scene. I should have saved that card as a surprise for the train. Now I decided to let Underwood think his conversation was beyond my German, because I guessed that ignorance might be my ticket to Berlin.

After the conductor was gone, Underwood smoked for several

minutes in heavy silence, suggesting all manner of sinister possibilities. This was going to be a very long ride. At last he said, "You may be right, but Oskar has disappeared."

"His body, you mean?" I tried to sound shocked.

"Body, yes. Mind and soul attached, I suspect."

"But I saw him dead."

"What do you know of death?" he asked, his voice turned hoarse with sudden anger. "I've seen more corpses before breakfast than you'll see in a lifetime." A thin line of sweat appeared on his forehead. I thought of Fritz's father, who traveled in the same mental circles, and figured it best to keep my mouth shut.

"The dogs," he said after a while in a normal tone of voice. "The dogs would have found him."

"They are active and enthusiastic," I agreed.

"They did not find him, ergo, he is not dead."

"I hope that you are right. Oskar is a fine boy."

Underwood took another tack, becoming confidential. "He was your friend. Did he know people on the island?"

An unexpected opening! I looked to the ceiling of our compartment, hoping for a particularly convincing lie. "Well, he had been to Rügen before. To Putbus. I think they had a family holiday there. I think they stayed not too far from our hostel."

Underwood exhaled a long column of smoke. "How would he have managed to get there?"

This was tricky territory. I shrugged and made a show of deep thought. "We came on bicycles."

"Too strenuous." He shook his head as if at his own carelessness and added, "If, as you say, he was badly hurt."

"The oberst has horses," I suggested finally. "Or someone might have moved his body. The boys are devoted to *der Bund* and to the oberst."

"You're not suggesting Oberst Weick had anything to do with the boy's injury."

"Who else would have weapons?"

"Impossible," Underwood said with a sniff. In another situation, I would have been amused at how the officer class automatically closed ranks. "But perhaps they drilled with weapons?"

"Wooden rifles. They're not apt to do much damage unless someone knocked him on the head with one."

He lifted his attaché case as if he'd made up his mind about something and set it on his knee. Official papers? Some work from the office? I didn't think so, and I didn't like the way he patted the leather and fiddled with the clasp as if struggling against an impulse to open it. After a few minutes, he said, "I know this route well. There are some woods, some bridges over the line, some dark sections. And quiet little stations where only the local stops. You are in an interesting position, Mr. Wood. You exist only in an embassy document. You were created *ex nihilo*, so to speak, and could disappear the same way."

"Fortunately, unlike Mr. Wood, Francis Bacon has family. Nan. Even an uncle."

"He's landed you in trouble," Underwood said. "I can't advise you to rely on him."

"Indeed. The oberst is his enemy."

"If so, your uncle is most likely dead." He paused. "But you might live."

"With the help of our embassy," I suggested. If he could keep up our charade, so could I.

"But only if you are honest with me. I don't believe that your friend Oskar Schafer is dead. What's more, I think you helped him leave the oberst's estate."

To be the focus of so much effort, Oskar must know a good deal about both Underwood and the oberst that wouldn't bear examination. I shook my head. "The last time I saw Oskar he was lying in a pool of blood."

"Then you are not useful to me," Underwood said.

I think that he would have opened the case if the conductor hadn't appeared at the door of our compartment. He was accompanied by a tall blond man with two suitcases and a messenger bag, holding a newspaper in his teeth. He dropped his assorted bags onto the seats, took the paper from his mouth, and thanked the conductor—he had gotten into the wrong compartment in the wrong carriage altogether.

Now he looked at his ticket and nodded to where I sat across from Underwood. I was in his seat, and, although Underwood gave me an evil look, I jumped up and immediately took the seat nearest the door and farthest from my companion.

The Swedish commercial traveler was apologetic. He always asked for a window seat facing the direction of travel, because of mild motion sickness. An inconvenience in his occupation.

"I should think so," I said. "But I don't mind switching. I might stand up for a while, anyway." With this I went into the corridor, pulled down one of the windows, and feigned a great interest in the passing scenery. Out of the corner of my eye, I saw the Swedish salesman chatting with Underwood. How about a chat with an assassin as a cure for nausea? *Concentrate, Francis!*

We slowed for a level crossing before accelerating again. Underwood was right that the local made a variety of stops, and now I recalled that, on our trip north, men had come on with carts of coffee and sandwiches between the larger stations. Could I make use of that? Or should I try locking myself in the lavatory? A tempting thought, but with the first-class compartment more than half-empty, I would be vulnerable alone at the end of the carriage. I decided that I was safer right where I was as long as the chatty Swede was in our compartment.

Was he going all the way to Berlin was the question. I had hopes until I heard him mention Prenzlau, a town about halfway. If that was his destination, I would be in trouble for the second half of the trip, and yes, it was to be Prenzlau, because he began explaining to Underwood, who I'm sure was charmed, that he had a consignment of ladies' stockings and some flatware to deliver there. The flatware was a new line, very cleanly designed.

I leaned back into the doorway and expressed genuine interest. I like to look at new things and modern designs. I would like to have seen the actual items, but he gave me a leaflet without opening his cases. I stood in the corridor, alternately studying the flatware designs—so different from the heavy, old-fashioned cutlery I was familiar with—and looking out for stations where I might make a quick exit.

Next up was Pasewalk. Let there be a man with a cart, who might block the aisle of our carriage and allow me to escape. As we slowed down approaching the station, I saw a few passengers waiting on the platform. None seemed bound for first class; however, I saw someone with a cart boarding farther down the platform. That was possibly better, for if he came to our carriage too far from a station, I would have nowhere to run but to the more crowded second- and third-class carriages.

Underwood would hardly take a shot in a crowd, but I wouldn't put it past him to summon the railway police on some pretext or attack me in some other way, relying on diplomatic immunity to keep him safe. I needed to get off at a station big enough to have a phone or a telegraph office and places to hide if Underwood was at my heels. Not easy to accomplish—in fact, nearly impossible. I leaned disconsolately against the window as we started to pull away. I was staring mindlessly at the tracks when the northbound train approached the station. I pulled my head back to avoid flying cinders, and I was ready to return to the compartment, when I saw Mac sitting at a window in the north-bound train; Miss Fallowfield must have received my telegram.

I thrust my hand out the open window, and at my frantic signal, he stood up in surprise. I drew my hand across my throat to signal my danger then lunged for the exit door of our carriage. We were already picking up speed when I pulled the emergency cord in the entryway. The squeal of the pneumatic brakes was followed immediately by the rattle of the carriage door sliding open with Underwood behind it.

I shoved a large suitcase across the doorway, dropped the exit-door window, fumbled for the latch, and as the door swung out, stepped off into space. I heard a pop behind me over the whoosh and rattle of the decelerating train before I landed with a terrible thump and rolled down the slope away from the line, over and over, finding rocks and roots and nettles at every revolution. Above, the clouds were revolving, dizzying white blobs against the blue sky. *Run, Francis.*

I rolled over. To my surprise, the ground was also in motion, spinning in a lazy rotation. I got to my hands and knees just the same and scuttled into some bushes. Up on the line, men were shouting back and forth, asking why the train had stopped, why the emergency brake had been pulled. I heard the rattle and bang of carriage doors opening and the huff of the engine and then my name called. That had to be Underwood. Ignoring the rippling ground and spinning clouds, I struggled further into the bushes, clutching a branch here and a tree there until I spotted a drainage culvert running under the track.

An oily trickle of water ran off into the brush, but when I got to the mouth of the pipe, I saw a glimmer of light from the other side, and with a glance toward the line—no silhouetted figures, no one sliding down the embankment—I scrambled into the culvert, a big, ribbed metal pipe, where I immediately slipped and fell on the slime and pebbles underfoot. For a moment, I couldn't move, then a trickle of icy water ran down my neck and I sat up. I had to reach the other side and hope that Mac had gotten off the northbound train and was looking for me.

Squatting under the low ceiling of the culvert, I started forward, helped by the ribs of the pipe, thinking *Please, no rats.* Dizzy as I was, I slipped several times, and it was just good luck that I had fallen and was thinking seriously of lying right where I was for the foreseeable future, when I heard footsteps amplified by the culvert. Someone was approaching the mouth of the pipe. I turned as slowly and carefully as I could, keeping my face just above the damp, muddy floor. Nothing. Was I hearing things? Perhaps railway officials walking far above me?

I waited, and I was almost ready to argue myself into moving forward again, when the light behind me was interrupted. Someone had come from my direction to stand at the mouth of the culvert. Someone tall, with lots of leg. "Francis?" someone called softly. "Are you there, Francis?"

I didn't answer. It was surely Underwood.

"The railway police will be here momentarily. If you're in there, you'd better come with me."

I flattened myself against the stones, my nose within a hair of breathing up the filthy water.

"I know you're there."

I raised my head a fraction. The light was now almost completely blocked. He must be crouched at the mouth of the culvert. He could not see me yet, but if he came in any farther, he would certainly find me, whether or not I tried to make my way to the far side of the line.

Suddenly a sound—a sinister pop—and something hard and metallic rattled off the roof of the culvert.

"Still hiding? Not a good idea," he said and fired off another shot. "You see, the sound is well muffled by the earth overhead. I can keep shooting until I hit you. Or you can come out now."

It was amazing how reasonable Underwood sounded given the circumstances, and I was beginning to think that I had no choice when he fired again, sending flakes of metal pinging down on me from the roof of the culvert. The pop and rattle of his shot was followed by an immense bang that made my ears ring. A shout of pain, another pop and rattle, another deafening bang, then silence—or rather an interior reverberation that momentarily took away all sound.

I raised my head. Once again the light at the end of the culvert was mostly blocked. Whoever was there had a weapon without the advantages of Underwood's silencer. "Francis? Can you hear me?"

"Mac?"

"Are you hurt?"

"Not shot. Bruised up."

"Get out the other end," he said. "I'm coming through."

I turned around and crawled toward the light on the east side. With a lot of bruises and what I guessed was a sprained ankle and something not quite right with one wrist, I made slow progress. Mac caught up with me before we reached the mouth of the culvert.

"Underwood?" I asked.

Mac gestured with his head. "With luck, they won't find him for a while. Wait," he said when I started outside. He looked out cautiously. I heard the rumble of a train overhead, and Mac touched my shoulder. Covered by the noise, we crawled out onto the grass. A dirt road ran along the fields, and I started limping toward the station, but Mac caught my arm.

"The railway police will be on alert, and you certainly look as if you've fallen out of a train. We'll find a barn or a shed to hide in until dark."

CHAPTER NINETEEN

I never intended to become a gentleman's outfitter," Mac said, as he opened a large brown paper parcel. A shirt, a sweater, heavy pants, a cap, and a leather jacket were inside, plus a change of underwear and socks. While he'd been off shopping and what he termed "reconnoitering," I'd been hiding in a roofless shed so chilly I couldn't remove my damp and filthy clothes without his help.

"What on earth were you doing in these, laddie?"

"Chimney sweeping," I said and explained how I had fooled the oberst and his fierce dogs. When I was dressed and beginning to warm up, I told him about Oskar. "He's in the hospital. I sent a telegram to his father, but I'm worried. The oberst is an important man on the island, and sooner or later he'll find out where Oskar is."

Mac sat down on a stone from the half-ruined wall and lit his pipe, an elaborate operation that required reaming the bowl and tamping it full of tobacco before the matches came out. I was used to the process. Mac used the pipe as a way of delaying decisions. Now he shook his head. "Above all else, the republic fears the Bolshies. As a result, they have been reluctant to crack down on the nationalist combat leagues and old front-line veterans' organizations. The left-wing fighters they go after; the right tends to get a free pass. That's just the way it is."

"Oskar could have died. He might have bled to death, and they would have passed it off as an accident. But it was Underwood who shot him, not the oberst."

"Leaving a boy who was a guest at his house to die does not make him much better," Mac observed.

"Then there's nothing we can do?"

"I didn't say that. It's risky, though. Whatever we do will make trouble for you without necessarily helping your friend. My best advice is to forget you ever met him."

"I can't do that. Besides, Oskar can put Underwood near the Eldorado the night Belinda was murdered. Wouldn't the police like to know about that? And Oskar's shooting. I can clear that up, too. Would that be enough—for them to maybe forget about the White Cat business?"

"The Prussian police don't forget anything," Mac said, "especially anything involving a violent death."

"They might want to prevent another one. Oskar has a bullet wound. Without me, it is just his word against the oberst's, and the oberst was going to blame me. If Oskar had died, I think he would have. He threatened me with the police unless I produced Uncle Lastings."

Mac thought this over. "Fortunately, for all concerned, Underwood is out of the picture. See he stays that way."

Although I was tempted to object, I nodded.

"So we might alert the local police," Mac suggested. "Or we might speak to your friend. He will have information useful to us. In exchange for protection."

"When?" I expected a consultation with the powers that be in Berlin and a confab with Miss Fallowfield and Harold, but I was wrong.

"Right now," Mac said. "I didn't get you all nicely kitted out just to ride back to Berlin."

"What if I'm spotted at the station?"

"We'll be on a different train with different conductors and police. Besides, you look quite respectable now, not at all like a lad who'd pull the emergency brake for fun. And remember, they are not looking for Underwood. Not yet. With luck, no one will find him for quite some time."

"But the embassy will miss him."

"The embassy has been informed. And about your assistance." With that, Mac got up, bundled my dirty clothes in the paper, and stuck it under his arm. "We'll dispose of these. Leave nothing behind wherever you hide."

"Right," I said. More useful advice that I hoped never to need again.

We walked along the track to the station, slowly, as my ankle had started to puff up. Dusk was falling before Mac secured our second-class tickets to Stralsund. The train was not expected for another two hours, and we spent the time in the waiting room, drinking bad coffee and eating stale sandwiches. Mac seemed the picture of tranquillity, smoking his pipe and reading a discarded newspaper. I don't know what bothered me more: the bizarre events of the past thirty-six hours or his nonchalant air.

"Were you really after Underwood?" I asked finally. "I mean, instead of looking for me."

"Both. I got lucky. Two birds with one stone." He took a closer look at me and added, "He would have killed you without thinking twice."

I nodded. "He shot Oskar. And probably Belinda."

"The only surprise is that he didn't kill your friend."

"Was my uncle his real target?"

Mac made a fuss of relighting his pipe before he said, "Everyone and his brother wants your uncle."

"But he's a con man. Don't you know that?"

"Even con men can have real information," Mac said.

Although it was late when we reached Stralsund, Mac insisted on going to the hospital right away, an urgency that made me nervous; I wasn't just imagining danger if the unflappable Mac was so serious. At the admitting desk, he asked if Oskar's father had arrived and claimed to be my friend's British uncle. "A far-flung family," he said, explaining that he had raced up from Berlin as soon as he heard the news. "A dreadful, dreadful business. And shot! Have the police been notified?" And so on. He secured a good deal of information, including the name of the officer who had taken a statement from Oskar.

"We'll maybe talk to him tomorrow," Mac said to me in an undertone as we entered the men's ward.

A single oil lamp cast a faint light down rows of beds screened by white canvas curtains. The ward was mostly empty, just the two old men I'd seen that morning who were now snoring contentedly. Oskar had been moved closer to the tall windows, and he was dozing, propped up on pillows, his face toward the town and the Baltic.

He stirred when he heard us approaching. "Francis! You're supposed to be in Berlin!" He sounded alarmed. Maybe he was expecting his father any minute, or maybe he was worried about my safety. I'd like to think that.

"This is Mac," I said. "He got me out of a jam. We needed to be sure you were safe."

"I'm going home tomorrow," he said. "With Father."

I patted his shoulder. Good-bye to the free and easy life in the "welcome circus of depravity"; hello to the stifling embrace of disapproval and respectability. No more nights on the town and maybe no more of *der Bund* and the *Wandervogel*, either. I could sympathize, I really could. "You will be safest at home. Until you get well."

"They say it will be some time. My head aches so." He moved restlessly, and I guessed that he was still feverish.

"Sleep," Mac said. "We will stay with you tonight and leave before your father arrives in the morning. We don't need to meet him."

Oskar gave a half smile at this and closed his eyes. Mac settled back in his chair, lit his pipe, and prepared to make a night of it, but I was suddenly overcome with weariness. I leaned forward, put my head in my arms at the side of Oskar's bed, and instantly fell asleep.

I woke up when Mac laid a warning hand on my back. I straightened up, disoriented, and he touched my lips for quiet. Someone was walking along the hallway outside the ward, and it was not the soft-footed nurses who I hazily remembered had looked in with their lamps and their watches to straighten pillows and to check pulses and temperatures. Mac had argued with one about our presence. She wanted the ward cleared. Mac said that a gunshot victim needed protection. He raised just enough doubt that she'd let us stay. This was someone else.

Mac reached over and drew the curtain carefully, then crouched on the floor behind Oskar's bed. I slid down beside him. A dark figure appeared against the hall light, then the glowing red dot of a cigarette held at an odd angle, and I felt my heart jumping. The oberst had discovered where Oskar was and had come to pay a visit. A friendly visit? I didn't think so, not at this time of night.

I started to rise, but Mac put his hand on my arm and shook his head. I heard footsteps, the sound of the curtain on the far side being drawn back cautiously, then a rustle like something being taken out of a paper parcel, and a smell. Oh, I recognized that! I remembered kerosene lamps and heaters in our nursery as a child.

Forgetting Mac and his warning, I leaped to my feet, shouting, "Stop! *Halten!* Stop!" just as a sheet of flame appeared with a flare and a whoosh over Oskar's bed. He woke with a scream, and I threw all my weight onto the near curtain, bringing it down over the flames and over Oskar. Careless of his injuries, I threw myself into the smells of burning fuel, linen, wool, and flesh, flailing my arms and trying to smother the flames. There was a scuffle beside the bed, but Mac was more than a match for Oberst Weick, whose false arm came loose to give the nurse who rushed in a bit of a turn.

"Help! Oskar needs help!" I cried, trying to disentangle myself from the curtain and to yank the smoldering sheets off the bed. I tumbled to the floor with the front of my sweater smoking and threatening flames, until a hefty nurse heaved a bucket of water over bed, sheets, and yours truly. Another nurse got the smoking bedcovers off Oskar and a third saw to the oberst, who was lying prone with Mac seated on his chest.

In short order, the police arrived. Oskar was moved to another bed, where they dressed his burns and put a new bandage on his leg, which was bleeding again. This time, a policeman sat guard. Both Mac and I had been summoned for an interview in a little storage room just off the ward. "Let me handle this," said Mac. I was quite willing to let him, and I must say he was very good. Maybe Harold was right that a top regimental sergeant, at least one with embassy connections, could manage anything.

I was presented as a juvenile on my own in Berlin: "A precarious life, gentlemen," Mac said. I had been befriended by a boy of good family—this was Oskar—who had important evidence to provide in a capital case. The boy was shot at the home of Oberst Weick, formerly a sponsor of their outing club. "Just how that shooting happened remains somewhat of a mystery," Mac said, "but his injuries were grossly neglected until Francis, here, managed to get his friend safely off the island and into the hospital."

You can believe that I glowed, if only momentarily, in the

light of friendship and heroism. Were the Kripos impressed? Yes, and, of course, they were grateful that our "timely action" had prevented serious injuries, even death. But—in my experience with police, there is always a *but*—there would be more questions, and the little matter of my stolen passport would have to be sorted out.

"Naturally," said the silken-tongued Mac. "The embassy will take care of that. And I will escort him back to Berlin immediately."

I think they likely wanted to ask Mac a thing or two—or three—but he was a bona fide member of the diplomatic corps with documents to prove it, and when he put his arm around my shoulders and claimed to be *in loco parentis* and what all else I don't remember, we were released with the caveat that I was to remain at my present address in Berlin for the foreseeable future. I thought that I might just get that clandestine run across the border yet.

By the time we walked past the ward, the mess had been tidied up, leaving only a faint oily, burned smell, and the ripple of nervous chatter passing between the beds of two old gaffers, who seemed to be arguing over who'd had the best view of the incident. I told Mac that I wanted to say good-bye to Oskar, as I thought it unlikely that I would ever see him again. When I stepped up to the officer in the doorway, he recognized us and nodded.

The curtains were closed around Oskar's bed, and when I peeked in, I saw that there were new bandages on both his arms. There was also a tall, stout man with a square face and little wire-rimmed glasses sitting beside the bed. He had Oskar's handsome features and fair complexion, and his hair was just touched with gray. In different circumstances, I'd have given him the eye, because he was just my type.

I nodded to him and said, "How are you, Oskar? How much damage?" and I put my hand on his shoulder.

Well, talk about an explosion. His father jumped up and began shouting, the heart of the message being to "get that little poofter away from my son!"

I was taken aback, and poor Oskar was speechless, but Mac put his arm around me and said, "Without this 'little poofter,' your son would have been dead twice over. You might think about that." He continued in quick and complicated German, probably revealing a lot more than Oskar had cared to about our adventures on the island and our vigil the night before.

"I'm leaving Germany," I said when Mac was finished, and Oskar's father had sat back down, looking as white and drained as he had looked red and angry just minutes before. I could see that he loved Oskar, although I knew his son didn't believe that. And I felt sad, because I realized that fathers and sons may love each other and long to be happy with each other yet not be able to manage. I suppose I might have taken a lesson from that.

Instead, I was mannerly, for though I would have liked to kiss him, I touched Oskar's hand instead. "Get well," I said. "Take care. And tell them about Belinda, who was brave, too."

Then I pushed the curtain aside and walked out. "I want to leave," I said to Mac. "One way or another, I've had enough of Berlin."

CHAPTER TWENTY

My Dear Nan,

You will be surprised when you get this letter, as I am writ-ing it from a second-class carriage on the SNCF! Yes! I am in France and, Nan, I am headed for Paris! The very best part is that I am traveling gratis, thanks to the Weimar Republic, which paid for my trip to the border, and to His Majesty's government, which has afforded me the rest. They would have sent me all the way to London, but with you being in Man-chester now—and I hope your newest old lady employer is not too much trouble—I thought I would save the benefactors some money and get off in Paris.

I know you are asking yourself if this official generosity is in gratitude for my assistance. Not exactly. Our govern-ment is grateful; the Germans feel my presence is undesir-able. Perhaps that is a natural difference of opinion given recent history.

• • •

The train rolled over some particularly rough points, and I stopped writing when my pen began to jitter across the paper. Nan admires good penmanship, and I try to send her my best. I was also uncertain how much of my recent adventure I should commit to paper. My friends at the embassy had been very clear that silence was expected: *Loose lips sink ships*, as the old slogan has it, and I had certainly seen Mac sink Underwood's ship without hesitation.

The Germans had also been enthusiastic about discretion. The oberst had heavyweight connections who weighed in with his war service and battle injuries and managed to shift ninety-nine percent of the blame to Aubrey Underwood, the missing British military attaché. There was some justice in that—and I certainly won't complain if only he'll stay missing!

At the same time, my dear Nan does love a good mystery— real, fictional, or something in between, which, I think, is the real nature of most accounts. I tried to frame another paragraph without success, and once the ink was dry—I'm never using a blotter again—I folded the still unfinished letter and got up to stretch my legs with a walk along the corridor.

The engine accelerated as we moved onto our new track, and I went swinging down the corridor, bouncing back and forth from the wall to the compartment doors. I was two carriages further on when the door of one compartment slid open by itself, and in surprise, I came to a dead halt and had to grab the doorframe to keep from sliding right into their seats.

He was sitting in the middle of a full compartment. Hair now a bright auburn that I did not find flattering. Ditto a narrow continental-style mustache. Open-necked shirt, blue jacket, not terribly well cut, and a beret. A beret for God's sake! His cigarette smelled like a Gauloises Bleu. He had everything French except the espadrilles, but I knew him right away. There sat my uncle Lastings, large as life.

"*Pardon, messieurs*," I said, recovering myself. I continued along the carriages, pausing outside the dining car, where I planted myself by a window to wait. I wanted an explanation for my uncle's extraordinary behavior, and I thought that a first-rate French meal would not go amiss, either. Sure enough, within a quarter of an hour, my uncle arrived, trailed by a plume of acrid French tobacco smoke—or, I should say, the man who had been my uncle but was now, as I was to discover, Monsieur Luc Pinot, an Alsatian exporter of wines based in Strasbourg with no relation to any Bacon anywhere on the globe.

For all that, he was friendly enough. "*Ah, mon ami*," he said in greeting and expressed his regret that the train was too crowded to allow us, as he put it, "to revisit pleasures past." Becoming French had obviously given a poetic slant to his conversation.

"Your hair is frightful," I said, which certainly hadn't topped the list of things I'd intended to say, but he was at once so himself and so different that I was momentarily at a loss. I recognized, as I had not when I first knew him, how completely he could inhabit a role, undoubtedly the knack that made him a successful con man. I realized that there might be little point in being angry with Monsieur Pinot, who was a totally different character from my feckless uncle.

"And where are you bound?" he asked, ignoring my remark.

"Paris."

"Paris! You lucky young dog! Paris does a man's heart good. You see if I'm not right."

"And you?"

"Just passing through," he said mysteriously. "But you look like you've thrived. And now you're off on a new adventure."

That was laying it on a bit thick. "I was deported."

He smirked at this. "Better yet. Saves the fare, don't you know. But don't tell me the good men of Weimar ponied up for Paris!"

"His Majesty's government gave me the rest."

With this, he clapped me on the shoulder. "*Mon ami!* If ever I see your respected father again, I will tell him he's raised a boy in a million. I will." He took another look at me. "And properly suited-up as well, though continental tailoring can't hold a candle to Saville Row. More's the pity," he added with a glance at his jacket.

"I landed on my feet," I admitted. Mac had kindly shopped again and replaced the badly singed sweater.

"What did I tell you? Didn't I say you'd be fine?"

"No thanks to you. I've been pursued by fanatics, nearly murdered twice, had one friend badly wounded, and another shot dead in an alley."

At this, Uncle crossed himself. He'd apparently gone over to Rome as well as to Paris. "Poor Arek," he said. "We met during the Great War. We must have a drink to absent friends." He motioned toward the dining car.

"You have funds?" I didn't fancy washing dishes on the SNCF.

"Ye of little faith. I have been entrusted with a project." He winked and opening the door to the dining car, waved me inside and patted me on the bum as I passed. In some ways, the Gallic edition of my uncle was unchanged.

White tablecloths, damask napkins, heavy cutlery—which, thanks to German and Swedish design, I now saw as hopelessly old-fashioned—and big leather-bound menus. "Shades of the Adlon," I said. The luxury of the hotel seemed years, not weeks, behind me.

But clearly my French uncle—that seemed the best way of thinking of him—did not want to revisit the Adlon. All right with me, at least for the moment; I was starving. Governments are fine with tickets, which are items that can be listed and inventoried and put in the books. They tend to skimp on food—especially food that exists only in prospect, like lunches, dinners, and breakfasts on a long train ride. I'd have been in a bad way if Miss Fallowfield had not packed a bag of sandwiches and a big slice of fruitcake.

"Champagne," said my French uncle. "We must have a champagne toast to Arek."

"To Belinda," I said. "As I knew him."

We touched glasses, and a quiet pall settled over our table, broken only by the arrival of the waiter with Chateaubriand for two, roast potatoes, and spring vegetables. By the time we were finished, I was halfway to forgiving him. Except for the White Cat.

"What did you do with the Webley?" I asked. We'd reached coffee and pastries. If he kicked me out of the carriage, I'd already have enjoyed a good meal.

He looked up sharply, and for a moment, Uncle Lastings as I had known him in Berlin reemerged. "That's bothered you."

"Of course it's bothered me. I had to keep ahead of the police, hide out, acquire false papers. And I was pursued by right-wing, combat-league fighters. I was cornered once and nearly beaten, and I was threatened with death on Rügen."

"A charming resort."

"More charming without fanatics with revolvers and savage dogs."

"Well," he said after I had told him a little more about my stay at the oberst's, "you see now what we're up against. They want to rebuild Germany in their own image—fanatical, militaristic, nationalistic. You wait and see, but I'm betting on them to do it."

"The men you shot—"

"Would have killed me. They intended to kill me and lured me there, unarmed, to do so. But first, they wanted my information, my contacts, and they might have gotten them, because I'm no bloody hero, and I've had enough pain to do me for a lifetime. So I took action."

"But you were running a racket. What sort of information would you have had?"

He thought for a moment. "Your friend Belinda—my friend Arek—hid in plain sight as a transvestite."

"He *was* a transvestite dancer."

"That's right, and a very good one, too. It was a role he enjoyed, but he was also a patriot and a soldier and a spy. What was more important, eh? The big hats or cozy tête-à-têtes with

German officers?" My French uncle looked away for a moment. "He was betrayed by one of us. That is very painful for me."

I nodded. That I did believe.

"What is so surprising about my activities? We are not one person, Francis, and we are not to be defined by what we wear or whom we fuck or the scam of the moment. Find what's important to you and hang on to it, and don't listen to any old men who want to send you over the top." With this, he waved to the waiter, paid the check, and left a generous tip. This time, he must be onto something good.

"I won't see you again," he said as we left the dining car. Then he stopped, legs braced against the sway, and, Gallic-style, kissed me on both cheeks. "*Bonne chance, mon ami*," he said and strode away down the corridor.

You will not guess, I wrote to Nan when I returned to my compartment, *whom I have just seen. And who treated me to a meal: He Who Cannot Be Named! Yes! I can only tell you that he is French now and off on some new scheme. I thought I was furious with him, because you know what a pickle he put me in, but you were right: Travel is an education and Berlin was certainly eye-opening. I have to thank He Who Cannot Be Named for that.*

What did I learn? That there are lots of people like me. And a whole world of pictures and designs to explore. Most of all, I learned that—Father's opinion notwithstanding—I'm a person of value who knows useful things, including some learned from the most unlikely people.

So there it is, Nan. I'm ready for Paris, the art center of the whole world. I'm going to learn good French and how to design wonderful things, and I'll discover a way to make a living for us both.

Love,

Francis

ABOUT THE AUTHOR

Janice Law is an acclaimed author of mystery fiction. The Watergate scandal inspired her to write her first novel, *The Big Payoff*, which introduced Anna Peters, a street-smart young woman who blackmails her boss, a corrupt oil executive. The novel was a success, winning an Edgar nomination, and Law went on to write eight more in the series. Law has written historical mysteries, standalone suspense, and, most recently, the Francis Bacon Mysteries, which include *The Prisoner of the Riviera*, winner of the 2013 Lambda Literary Gay Mystery Award. She lives and writes in Connecticut.

THE FRANCIS BACON MYSTERIES

FROM MYSTERIOUSPRESS.COM
AND OPEN ROAD MEDIA

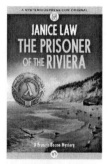

Available wherever ebooks are sold

MYSTERIOUSPRESS.COM

OPEN ROAD
INTEGRATED MEDIA

MYSTERIOUSPRESS.COM

Otto Penzler, owner of the Mysterious Bookshop in Manhattan, founded the Mysterious Press in 1975. Penzler quickly became known for his outstanding selection of mystery, crime, and suspense books, both from his imprint and in his store. The imprint was devoted to printing the best books in these genres, using fine paper and top dust-jacket artists, as well as offering many limited, signed editions.

Now the Mysterious Press has gone digital, publishing ebooks through **MysteriousPress.com**.

MysteriousPress.com offers readers essential noir and suspense fiction, hard-boiled crime novels, and the latest thrillers from both debut authors and mystery masters. Discover classics and new voices, all from one legendary source.

FIND OUT MORE AT

WWW.MYSTERIOUSPRESS.COM

FOLLOW US:

@emysteries and Facebook.com/MysteriousPressCom

MysteriousPress.com is one of a select group of publishing partners of Open Road Integrated Media, Inc.

THe MYSTeRIOUS BOOKSHOP, founded in 1979, is located in Manhattan's Tribeca neighborhood. It is the oldest and largest mystery-specialty bookstore in America.

The shop stocks the finest selection of new mystery hardcovers, paperbacks, and periodicals. It also features a superb collection of signed modern first editions, rare and collectable works, and Sherlock Holmes titles. The bookshop issues a free monthly newsletter highlighting its book clubs, new releases, events, and recently acquired books.

58 Warren Street
info@mysteriousbookshop.com
(212) 587-1011
Monday through Saturday
11:00 a.m. to 7:00 p.m.

FIND OUT MORe AT:

www.mysteriousbookshop.com

FOLLOW US:

@TheMysterious and Facebook.com/MysteriousBookshop

CPSIA information can be obtained at www.ICGtesting.com
Printed in the USA
BVOW05s0931270316

441829BV00001B/1/P